ANNE MATHER

The Baby Gambit

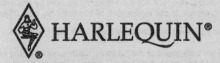

HARLEQUIN®

TORONTO • NEW YORK • LONDON
AMSTERDAM • PARIS • SYDNEY • HAMBURG
STOCKHOLM • ATHENS • TOKYO • MILAN • MADRID
PRAGUE • WARSAW • BUDAPEST • AUCKLAND

ISBN 0-373-12055-9

THE BABY GAMBIT

First North American Publication 1999.

Copyright © 1999 by Anne Mather.

All rights reserved. Except for use in any review, the reproduction or
utilization of this work in whole or in part in any form by any electronic,
mechanical or other means, now known or hereafter invented, including
xerography, photocopying and recording, or in any information storage
or retrieval system, is forbidden without the written permission of the
publisher, Harlequin Enterprises Limited, 225 Duncan Mill Road,
Don Mills, Ontario, Canada M3B 3K9.

All characters in this book have no existence outside the imagination of
the author and have no relation whatsoever to anyone bearing the same
name or names. They are not even distantly inspired by any individual
known or unknown to the author, and all incidents are pure invention.

This edition published by arrangement with Harlequin Books S.A.

® and TM are trademarks of the publisher. Trademarks indicated with
® are registered in the United States Patent and Trademark Office, the
Canadian Trade Marks Office and in other countries.

Visit us at www.romance.net

Printed in U.S.A.

CHAPTER ONE

GRACE stepped out onto the balcony of the *appartamento* and took her first real look at the blue waters of the bay. Breathing deeply, the shiver that shook her frame at that moment was induced more by excitement and anticipation than by the slight coolness of the morning air. She was here, she thought. She was in Italy. And for the next two weeks she had nothing more momentous to think about than what she was going to do to fill her time.

Below the faded grandeur of the old apartment building, the terraced slopes of Portofalco zigzagged their way down to the harbour. Portofalco was not the most well-known or the most exclusive resort on this section of the Ligurian coast, but it was one of the prettiest, and Julia had told her that many of its wealthier visitors came back year after year.

And she should know, conceded Grace sagely, resting her elbows on the balcony rail and feeling the chill of wrought iron against her slim bare arms. As yet, this corner of the Villa Modena was still in shadow, but she guessed that when the sun rose higher this balcony would be a veritable sun-trap, and she'd be grateful for the louvred shutters that bracketed every window.

She wondered what time Julia would get back from Valle di Falco. Her friend, who lived all year in the small apartment, and who worked in one of the larger hotels along the coast, was away for the weekend, and Grace didn't expect her back until tomorrow. But she didn't mind. When she'd accepted Julia's invitation to come here and stay with her, it had been on the understanding that her friend should not feel she had to entertain her while she was here. Julia had

5

a busy social life, she knew, but Grace hoped not to get involved.

The two women had known one another since their college days, and although they hadn't seen much of one another since Julia had come to live in Italy two years ago they'd kept in touch. There'd always been a casual familiarity between them that didn't seem to be affected by the passage of time, which was why Grace had been grateful for the invitation, knowing that with Julia she wouldn't be expected to do anything.

And all she really wanted to do was rest, she conceded ruefully, even if it had taken a bout of pneumonia to convince her of the fact. Holding down two jobs, and trying to look after her invalid mother into the bargain, had been exhausting, but she hadn't realised she was neglecting her health until she'd collapsed.

It all seemed so obvious in retrospect, but at the time there didn't seem to be anything else she could do. She was the only member of her family who was unmarried; therefore it was up to her to look after her mother, and she'd given up her own apartment and moved back into her mother's house in Brighton.

And that was when life had become really hectic. Travelling up to London every day, trying to maintain her job at the museum, had been hard enough, but going out most evenings, working behind the bar at the local pub to supplement her income, had ultimately proved too much. She'd caught a bad cold, not a serious one, she'd assured herself, but it had rapidly developed into something else.

It had taken a stay in hospital to convince her that she couldn't go on looking after her mother alone, with only a home help during the day to support her. So with some persuasion by a friendly doctor her two younger sisters had agreed to share the responsibility. But they had husbands and young families, and Grace guessed their assistance would only be temporary, so she intended to make the most of this holiday to build up her strength.

The alternative was to put her mother into a home, and she didn't want that. Grace loved her mother dearly and it wasn't her fault that she'd developed a crippling form of osteoarthritis only a couple of years after Grace had got her doctorate and started work at the museum. She'd managed to look after herself to begin with, but gradually, over the years, her condition had deteriorated. Now she could only get about in a wheelchair, and there'd been no way Grace could afford to provide professional care on her salary.

So, she had gone back to live at home. Grace had already begun to believe that she'd never get married anyway, so it was no great hardship. She was the perennial spinster, she thought drily, eschewing the more popular description of a bachelor girl. Euphemisms were all very well, but the fact was she'd given up believing she was ever going to meet a man who was not intimidated by either her appearance or her intellect. At a little under six feet in height, and with the kind of Junoesque figure most women would die for, Grace had always considered herself an oddity. She saw nothing attractive about her full breasts and generously curved hips and she kept her hair long and severely braided to quell the uncontrollable urge it had to tumble in a riotous tangle of silvery blonde curls about her heart-shaped face.

Of course, she hadn't always been so cynical. When she was at college, and boys of her own age were falling over themselves to go out with her, she'd imagined that one day she'd fall in love and get married and live happily ever after. She'd been in no hurry to give up her single state, but the prospect had always been there, like a friendly beacon on the horizon.

It hadn't happened.

She'd eventually realised that most of the men she dated wanted only one thing and that was to get her into bed. They didn't seem either willing or capable of looking beyond the 'dumb blonde' image she presented to the world to the slightly shy and intelligent woman behind the sexy façade. The men who might have appealed to her were put off by her appearance. In their own way, they had judged her, too, and by the time she'd realised that the girls who found lasting relationships didn't look like her she'd lost both her innocence and her trust.

She'd still dated from time to time, of course, but she'd changed, and she'd soon grown tired of defending her celibate state to men who still seemed to think that with her looks she must be desperate for sex. The truth was, her experiences of sex had not been particularly enjoyable, and she saw no sense in stressing herself over something she didn't even like.

These days she was much more philosophical, she reflected comfortably, glancing down as the breeze that blew off the distant water caused the short hem of her nightshirt to flutter about her shapely thighs. She was thirty-four, with no prospect of a steady relationship in sight, and she'd finally come to the conclusion that she preferred it that way.

She sighed contentedly, feeling grateful that Julia had come to the rescue with the offer of this chance to share her apartment for two weeks. Booking a holiday at the height of the tourist season could have proved difficult, and she preferred the anonymity of private accommodation to the obvious disadvantages of a hotel. All she'd wanted was somewhere warm and sunny, with nothing to do but laze the days away.

'I won't be around much, I'm afraid,' Julia had said, when Grace had phoned her from the hospital to tell her what was going on. 'This is the busiest time of the year for me, but you're welcome to stay as long as you like. Portofalco is a pretty place, and if you get bored you can always hire a car and go exploring.'

Grace had assured her that it sounded like heaven and consequently here she was, the morning after her arrival, standing on Julia's balcony just drinking in the view. And it was quite a view, she conceded, with the Bay of Portofalco below her, and the curve of the mainland sweeping round to Viareggio and beyond.

She took a deep breath, her nose wrinkling at the mingled perfumes of the flowers that rose from the walled garden beneath the balcony. It wasn't much of a garden, really, and it had been sadly neglected, but the tangled scents of jasmine and verbena, and the roses that clung tenaciously to the crumbling walls, were a heady delight. Somehow, even the overgrown garden had an enchanted air about it, hinting of assignations beside the lichen-studded fountain whose basin was crumbling, too.

Turning away from the view, Grace decided it was time she took a shower and got dressed. When she'd arrived the night before, she'd been too tired to do anything more than phone her mother to assure her she'd arrived safely, and strip off her clothes and tumble into bed. But it was eight o'clock in the morning now and her unpacking beckoned. Then breakfast, she thought with some anticipation, remembering that Julia had told her there was a bakery just down the street. The prospect of warm rolls and flaky pastries was appealing, and she strode across the rather over-furnished *salotto* into the bathroom beyond.

Fifteen minutes later, she felt considerably more energetic, and although she'd decided to put off her unpacking until later she put on a pair of cream silk shorts and a matching tank top to make her feel more like a holiday-maker. A glance in the bathroom mirror assured her that her mouth required little in the way of cosmetics, and she merely added a trace of blusher to give colour to her pale cheeks.

Her face was only too familiar to her and therefore nothing out of the ordinary, so that when she scraped back her hair into its usual braid and several rebellious loose ends curled about her temples she saw only the untidiness of it. But the old caretaker who looked after the building, and who had given her the key Julia had left for her the night before, greeted her with genuine pleasure, his rheumy old eyes glinting appreciatively as he watched her saunter off down the cobbled street.

The Villa Modena—Grace privately thought its title was rather flattering—stood halfway down a narrow street of similar dwellings. The street, the Via Cortese, wound up from the harbour, and she could see snatches of blue, blue water between vine-hung walls and over colour-washed roofs. Every now and then, an opening offered a tantalising view of the bay, with the masts of yachts moored at the jetty moving gently on the incoming tide.

She smelled the bakery before she reached it, the delicious aroma of newly baked bread making her mouth water. Which was unusual for her considering she hadn't had much of an appetite at all since her illness, and she looked forward to enjoying a warm roll with the pot of coffee she'd left on the hotplate at the apartment.

The baker was red-cheeked and friendly, dismissing Grace's attempts to make herself understood with a cheerful shake of his head. '*Va bene, signorina,*' he assured her firmly. 'I have the English, *no*?' He smiled and gestured to the impressive array of bread available. 'You tell me what you like.'

'*Grazie.*' Grace gave him an apologetic smile. 'I'm not very good at learning languages, I'm afraid. But I'm staying for two weeks, so perhaps my Italian will improve.'

'*Prego!*' The man laughed. 'We *Italianos* will always forgive a beautiful woman, sì?'

Grace's lips thinned a little at the familiar compliment, but she accepted his flattery good-humouredly. 'You're very kind,' she said, pointing to a batch of crusty rolls. 'I'll have three of those, please, and two pastries. *Grazie!*'

She was pocketing her change before taking the bag of sweet-smelling pastries from his hand when, to her relief, the arrival of another customer distracted him. '*A domani,*' he called after her. 'Until tomorrow.' And Grace lifted a hand in reluctant acknowledgement as she made her escape.

She could smell the pot of coffee as soon as she opened the door. The apartment, which was situated on the second floor of the villa, opened directly into the living room, with the tiny kitchenette occupying an alcove off the living area. A trellis of climbing greenery set in an earthenware container provided an impromptu screen, with a narrow counter at right angles to it where Julia evidently took her meals when she was at home.

Grace found some low-fat butter substitute in the small fridge and spread some on one of the warm rolls. Then, after pouring herself a mug of the strong black coffee, she perched on one of the tall stools that were pushed against the bar to enjoy her meal.

She was flicking idly through an old copy of *Figaro* when someone knocked at the door. She turned at once, guessing it was a visitor for Julia who didn't know she was away. Hopefully, not a man, she thought ruefully, wiping a crumb from her lip. If she remembered correctly, Julia was spending the weekend with the current man in her life and, judging by her excitement when she'd mentioned him to Grace, it seemed that she hoped that this might be the one.

Grace grimaced. Her friend was much less cynical than she was. Even with a failed marriage behind her, Julia had still maintained that there was a man out there somewhere just waiting for her to come along. Perhaps this weekend's *amoroso*, as they said in Italy, was different. Grace begged leave to reserve judgement until she'd met the man for herself.

But she was wasting time. As another knock sounded at the door, she slid off the stool and crossed the room. It could just be the old caretaker, she surmised. Perhaps he'd smelled the appetising aroma of the coffee, and found some excuse to come up here so that she could offer him a cup. If so, he was going to be disappointed. She had no intention of inviting any strange man into the apartment.

But the man standing outside was not the caretaker. 'Miss Horton?' he asked, and although she was sure he was Italian there was no trace of an accent in his low, attractive voice.

There was a suitcase standing beside him, but Grace registered this only peripherally as she gazed at one of the few men who could give her a few inches in height. He was tall, extremely dark both in hair and skin, with a lean yet obviously muscular body. He was certainly one of the most attractive men she'd ever seen, yet no one, not even his mother, could have called him handsome.

His eyes—dark eyes, what else? she mocked herself sardonically—were too deeply set, with hooded lids and thick black lashes hiding their expression. His cheekbones were harshly carved in a face that looked more inclined to severity than humour. Yet his mouth belied that conclusion, she reflected. Thin-lipped, perhaps, but with an obvious tendency towards laughter. Right now, she suspected he was laughing at her, and she felt a sharp tug of resentment at the thought.

'Yes?' she said coolly, unhappily aware that she had been staring at him far longer than she should have. She registered the suitcase properly now, propped beside one loafer-clad foot. A foot without any sock, she appended cynically, below loose-fitting cotton trousers that only hinted at the powerful thighs that flexed beneath.

Who was he? she wondered irritably. Surely Julia hadn't invited someone else to stay to keep her company. Yet how else had he known her name? 'Can I help you?' she asked, aware of the violent urge she had to scream.

He bent and picked up the suitcase. 'I just want to leave this for Julia,' he said, as Grace was preparing herself to block his way. 'It's hers,' he explained, evidently recognising her hostility. 'She was my guest last evening and I agreed to deliver it back to her apartment.'

Grace's jaw dropped. 'You mean, you're—'

'Matteo di Falco,' he introduced himself easily as she stepped aside to allow him to set the suitcase down inside the door. 'Unfortunately, Julia was obliged to cut the weekend short. She had to get back to the hotel.'

'She did?' Grace knew she sounded blank, but she couldn't help it.

'They phoned this morning,' he agreed, straightening. 'There has been some illness and they are short of staff. They asked if she could return immediately.' He shrugged his shoulders, broad beneath the lightweight jacket he was wearing over a white tee shirt. '*Cosi sia!* So be it.'

Grace nodded. 'Well—thank you for letting me know.'

His thin lips twisted. 'It was my pleasure.'

She doubted it was, but he was too polite to say otherwise. 'Um—thanks, anyway. I'm sorry if it's spoiled your weekend.'

'I will survive,' he assured her drily, and she wondered what he really thought of her. 'Enjoy your holiday, Miss Horton. *Arrivederci!*'

He turned away without further ado, strolling back along the gallery that overlooked the inner courtyard of the villa with indolent grace. All the apartments opened onto similar galleries, a flight of worn marble stairs giving access to the lower floors, and Grace waited until he'd started down the stairs before going back into the apartment and closing the door.

She leaned against the door for a moment, before taking a deep breath and walking into the kitchen. But as she edged back onto the stool and raised her mug of coffee to her lips she found Matteo di Falco's image refused to be displaced.

She shook her head, a moan that was half laughter, half disgust escaping her throat. So that was Julia's latest heart-throb, she thought self-derisively. And she'd behaved as if she'd never seen a man before.

She pushed the half-eaten roll aside and propped her elbows on the counter. She had to admit, Julia hadn't been exaggerating this time. What was the expression she'd used? Drop-dead gorgeous? Well, he was certainly that, and unlikely to be any more reliable than the rest.

By the time she'd cleared her breakfast dishes away and

unpacked, it was nearly midday. She had wondered if Julia might ring to confirm her change of plans, but she didn't, so after making sure the apartment was tidy Grace decided to go and explore the town.

It was much hotter now, the early summer sun baking the walls of the old buildings so that there was little coolness in their shade. Grace was halfway down to the harbour when she began to doubt the sense in what she was doing, but she decided it would be easier to go on than to turn back.

Besides, there were cafés appearing at every corner, and tables set beneath canvas awnings dotted the small promenade. There were plenty of people about, but it wasn't difficult to find a table in a shady corner, and she ordered a chilled glass of Campari and soda while she studied the menu.

There was a delightful breeze blowing off the water, and her eyes were continually drawn to the busy quay, where fishing boats vied for space among sleek yachts and sailing dinghies. Enviably tanned men and women were standing about in groups, modelling the latest styles in designer gear, or sunning themselves on the decks of gleaming motor cruisers anchored in the bay.

At the end of a short pier, a ferry was boarding, taking passengers to other resorts along the coast, and Grace mused that the whole scene looked as if it had been lifted from the pages of a glossy holiday brochure. So why was it that when the waiter appeared to take her order she felt so alone suddenly? And why did she find herself wishing that there was still a man in her life, too?

'I'll have the risotto salad,' she told the waiter, pointing out her choice just in case he didn't understand what she meant.

'Ah, *bene*,' he said, smiling approvingly. 'You like the *vino*, *sì*?'

'No, thank you.' Grace covered her glass with her hand

and smiled to soften her refusal. 'Just the salad, if you don't mind.'

'Okay, *signora*.'

The man inclined his head resignedly, and Grace wondered if his use of the more formal salutation was a sign that she was looking old.

She grimaced. There was no doubt that the waiter was considerably younger than she was. Twelve years, at least, she decided drily, and then caught him watching her as he punched the code for her order into the till.

She turned her head away at once, anxious to avoid him thinking she was interested in him. But, as she stared at the view, she wondered when she'd stopped being flattered by a stranger's attention; when she'd become so wary of a man's motives that she froze out every male she met.

The suspicion that the waiter was still watching her caused her to glance around again, but the young man was nowhere to be seen. Evidently, he had gone to collect someone else's order and she decided she must be getting paranoid, sensing eyes upon her when there weren't any there.

Yet…

A shiver rippled down her spine as the uneasy feeling of being scrutinised persisted, and she almost jumped out of her skin when a low masculine voice spoke just above her head. 'We meet again, Miss Horton.' Matteo di Falco's casual greeting was polite, but detached, and she supposed she couldn't blame him after the way she'd treated him before.

'Oh—' She looked up at him awkwardly. 'Um—hello.' A swift glance up and down the promenade ascertained the fact that he was alone, too. She forced a smile. 'I'm just trying to keep out of the sun.'

'So I see.' Long-fingered hands dipped into the pockets at the waistline of his trousers. '*Bene*, enjoy your meal.'

Grace took a deep breath. 'Are—are you having lunch—um—*signore*?' she asked, with rather more warmth than she'd shown thus far, and his thin lips parted to allow his tongue access to the corner of his mouth.

'What is it you English say?' he asked, dark humour evident in the depths of his lazy eyes. 'As if you care, *no*?' he suggested wryly. Then, as if regretting his own irony, he added, 'But to answer your question, no. I was simply exchanging a few words with a colleague, when I saw you sitting here, alone.'

Grace's lips tightened at the implied vote of sympathy, and before she could stop herself she said, 'I enjoy my own company, as it happens.'

'I am sure you do,' he answered smoothly, but despite the courtesy of his words Grace felt a hot wave of colour envelop her cheeks. For God's sake, she thought crossly, he would think she was a complete idiot. Not only shrewish, but gauche as well.

'I didn't mean that the way it sounded,' she found herself protesting hurriedly, but she saw at once that her efforts to excuse herself had fallen on stony ground.

'Oh, I'm sure you did, Miss Horton,' he countered flatly. 'Once again, please accept my good wishes.' He glanced up at the awning. 'You've chosen well. The food here is some of the best in town.'

CHAPTER TWO

GRACE was stir-frying a pan of vegetables when Julia arrived home.

After lunch at the quayside café, she'd spent some time looking round the little town that crowded the harbour, and she hadn't been able to resist buying some of the fresh fruit and other produce she'd found displayed in the small shops. There had been so many varieties of peaches and plums and apricots, as well as the more familiar things such as beans and peas, sweet corn and peppers, which gave off such an appetising aroma as they simmered in the pan.

If she'd wondered whether she might run into Matteo di Falco again, that was something she preferred not to think about. But she couldn't deny that her eyes had been drawn to every tall dark man she'd seen. Still, whatever he'd been doing before he'd spoken to her at the café, he was apparently no longer in Portofalco, and she'd decided she was lucky not to have to deal with him again.

But it was good to see Julia, and Grace removed the pan from the heat before going to meet her friend. They hugged and exchanged greetings, before Julia subsided somewhat gratefully onto one of the stools that flanked the breakfast bar. 'I'm beat!' she exclaimed, pulling a wry face. She nodded towards the stove. 'But I'm glad to see you're making yourself at home.'

Grace grimaced. 'I hoped you wouldn't mind. I didn't know if you'd be coming home, or what time, but I thought if you did you wouldn't want to go out for a meal. So I've made enough for two.'

'Great,' said Julia, putting her elbow on the bar and resting her head on her hand. 'I'm sorry I couldn't be here when you arrived.' She pulled a face. 'I had my weekend all planned.'

'But you had to cut it short,' murmured Grace sympathetically, taking the bottle of wine she'd opened earlier from the fridge. She poured a glass and pushed it towards Julia. 'Well, you can relax now. Supper's almost ready.'

'Thanks.'

Julia sipped the wine with evident enjoyment, and as she did so Grace took a moment to glance at her friend. Was it only the fact that she'd had to put in these extra hours that had made her look so weary? Or was there some other problem troubling her? If she waited long enough, she guessed Julia would tell her what it was.

'So, how are you?' Julia enquired now, straightening her back and resting both arms on the counter. 'I must say you look pretty good, considering.'

Grace glanced with mock indignation over her shoulder. 'Talk about being damned with faint praise,' she said, wrinkling her nose.

'You know what I mean,' insisted Julia. 'I expected you to look all wan and haggard-eyed. Instead of which, it's me who looks as if I've been on a bender for a week.'

'I wouldn't say that.' Despite her obvious weariness, Julia still possessed the gamine charm she'd had when they were students. Smaller than her friend, Julia had always been excessively slender, with short blonde hair that was presently shaped to curl confidingly in towards her pointed chin. 'It was a shame the hotel knew where to contact you. If they hadn't, I suppose they'd have had to call on someone else.'

'Yeah.' Julia grimaced. 'That was my fault. If I hadn't been bragging about going to Valle di Falco for the weekend, they wouldn't have known where I was. But it's not every day that you get to meet a real *marchesa*, and I couldn't resist telling everyone that I was going to stay at the di Falco villa.'

'Ah.' Grace could feel a certain tightness in her throat.

'Does that mean that—that Signor di Falco is really a *marchese*?'

'Matteo?' Julia took a sip of her wine, but Grace could see that her blue eyes had become a little dreamy. 'Well, yes, he is. But these days, like lots of other Italian aristo-crats, he doesn't use his title.'

Grace was glad of the excuse of attending to the vege-tables to turn back to the stove. So, Matteo di Falco was really the Marchese di Falco. Her tongue circled her upper lip. Things just seemed to get worse and worse. What must he have thought of her? She just hoped he didn't tell Julia what she'd said.

'Anyway,' Julia went on now, and Grace could hear the animation in her voice, 'you haven't told me what you thought of him. Matt, I mean. He did fetch my suitcase, didn't he?'

'Oh, yes. He brought it.' Grace judged herself capable of speaking casually, and turned to take a plate of fresh shrimp out of the fridge. If Julia thought she was flushed, she would probably put it down to the heat emanating from the vegetables. 'He arrived about mid-morning. He ex-plained you'd been summoned back to the hotel.'

Julia nodded. 'So what did you think?' she persisted ea-gerly. 'Come on, Grace; don't you think he's something else?' She shook her head. 'I still can't get over the fact that he's interested in me. It's the real thing this time, girl. I'm sure of it.'

Grace expelled a breath. 'He seemed—very nice.'

'Very *nice*!' Julia snorted, her weariness apparently for-gotten. 'Can't you do better than that? When I look at him, "nice" is not an epithet that instantly springs to mind!'

'All right, he's everything you said he was,' conceded Grace unwillingly, tipping the uncooked shrimp into the pan and giving them a rather energetic stir. 'The food's almost ready. Shall we eat in here? Or would you rather I set the table in the living room?'

Julia looked as if she would have preferred to continue

their discussion of Matteo di Falco, but after swallowing the remainder of the wine in her glass she seemed to think better of it. 'Let's just eat here,' she said, helping herself to more wine. 'Mmm, it smells delicious. I could get used to this.'

Happily, the conversation became more general as they consumed the meal, but Julia wanted to know how her friend had come to neglect her health. She expressed her own outrage that Grace's sisters should have had to be prevailed upon to help, showing little sympathy for their responsibilities towards their own families.

'She's their mother, too,' she reminded Grace sagely, getting up to help her friend with the dishes. 'And they don't work, remember? They probably have far more free time than you.'

Grace admitted that that was a possibility, but she had grown so used to being regarded as the fall girl that it was hard to blame anyone else. Besides, she had never considered what she did as a burden before. It was only when she was taken ill herself that she'd begun to realise that she might be doing too much.

'Anyway, you're here now, and I don't want you to feel that I expect you to look after me while you're convalescing,' declared Julia, putting their clean plates back into the cupboard. 'I mean, this has been quite a treat, having a meal prepared for me and all, but I'm used to picking up something on my way home if I haven't eaten, and, of course, I am out several nights a week.'

'That's okay.' Grace dried her hands and watched her friend spooning coffee into the filter before retiring to the living area beyond the screen of climbing plants. 'I'm looking forward to relaxing: reading some books, catching up on my correspondence, that sort of thing. Even a little sunbathing,' she added as Julia carried the tray containing the coffee into the room. 'As I said when you invited me here, I don't want to interfere in your life.'

'As if.' Julia pulled a face and subsided onto the sofa

with a grateful sigh. 'Ah, that's better,' she said, kicking off her shoes and curling her toes into the rug. Then she added, 'Your being here is not a problem, Grace. Not to me, anyway. I've wanted you to come out here for ages; you know that. Only you've always had an excuse before.'

Grace took the armchair opposite her friend, and lifted her shoulders in an apologetic shrug. 'It hasn't always been easy—' she began, and Julia nodded as she pulled herself upright again and reached for the coffee pot.

'Your mother,' she agreed. 'I know. But I'm glad I can be of help now. And it makes a change to have an English person to talk to.'

Grace hesitated and then, conceding to herself that she had been a little offhand about Julia's boyfriend before, she made an effort to make amends. 'Um—Matteo—' she grimaced at her pronunciation '—speaks very good English, doesn't he? Or does he only speak his own language with you?'

Julia waited until she'd handed her friend a cup of coffee and had got comfortable again on the sofa before replying. 'As a matter of fact, Matt is partly English,' she explained, propping her feet on the brass-topped table between them. 'The *marchesa* I spoke of—she's English, you see. She married Matt's grandfather—oh, it must be over sixty years ago now. Of course—' she pulled a wry face '—she's more Italian than he is. Do you know, she never once addressed me in English while I was staying at the villa? Matt says she hardly ever uses her native language any more.'

Grace frowned. 'You met his grandmother?' she asked in surprise. 'Not his parents?'

'His parents are dead.' Julia gazed somewhat consideringly into space before going on. 'Matt's father was a keen skier, and he and his wife were killed in an avalanche near Courmayeur when Matt was just a baby.' She pulled her gaze back to her friend. 'His grandparents brought him up.'

'I'm sorry.'

Grace spoke sincerely, and Julia gave her a rueful look.

'Yes, so am I. Matt's grandfather is dead now, but the old lady's quite a tartar. I don't think her attitudes have altered since the Second World War!'

Grace smiled. 'Aren't you being a little unkind? Just because she chooses to speak the language she's most accustomed to, you're accusing her of being out of date.'

'Well, it wasn't just that.' Julia spoke defensively. 'She made me feel as if I wasn't welcome there.' She grimaced. 'To be honest, I wasn't exactly disappointed when I got that call from the Continental. I think she needs a little more time to get used to the idea that Matt and I are a couple. It'll be easier next time. I'll make sure I've genned up on wine-growing and Italian history before I go.'

Grace's eyes widened. 'They own a vineyard?' She shook her head. She'd put Matteo di Falco down as a wealthy playboy and nothing more.

'They own the valley,' said Julia repressively. 'And I don't think the *marchesa* really approved of Matt getting involved in a commercial enterprise like making wine. As I said before, she's an anachronism, Grace. Without Matt's efforts, they'd have had to sell out years ago.'

Grace absorbed what Julia had said. 'So—this is Matteo's vineyard?'

'Vine*yards*,' Julia corrected her firmly. 'They've always grown grapes in the Valle di Falco, of course, but it was his idea to turn it into a real business.'

'I see.' Grace was impressed.

'Anyway, that's enough about boring things like making money,' said Julia, looking more cheerful. 'Let's talk about what you really thought of Matt. Don't you think we'll make a stunning couple?'

'Stunning,' echoed Grace obediently, but she couldn't help wondering if Julia wasn't being a little premature with her plans. Even if Matteo di Falco worked for his living, he was an aristocrat first and foremost, and Grace hoped her friend wouldn't be too disappointed if their relationship didn't work out.

'You're very cagey,' said Julia now, sensing that Grace wasn't being entirely honest, and Grace decided quickly that it was really nothing to do with her.

'Not at all,' she protested, reaching for her coffee to avoid Julia's knowing stare. 'Um—how long have you known him? How did you meet?'

Julia still looked doubtful, but she accepted the evasion, much to Grace's relief. 'We met at a reception in Florence,' she replied. 'One of the guests who was staying at the hotel had tickets for a special evening exhibition of Renaissance art. Of course, we're not supposed to fraternise with the guests, but he wasn't able to attend the reception, so he offered his tickets to me.' She shook her head. 'Not that I'm mad about art or anything like that, but there was going to be wine and canapés, stuff like that, and Maria and I— Maria's another of the receptionists at the hotel, like me— we thought it might be worth a look.'

'And it was,' commented Grace drily, and Julia gave a rueful grin.

'Wasn't it just?' she agreed eagerly. 'I saw Matt the minute I walked in.' She smiled reminiscently. 'It turned out that it was his cousin who owned the gallery, and he'd only agreed to come along to show some support.'

Grace nodded. 'So how did you wangle an introduction?'

'I didn't.' Julia looked smug. 'I introduced myself. I had the ideal opportunity, you see. Signor Massina—he was the guest who gave me the tickets—asked me to offer Carlo— that's the name of Matt's cousin—his apologies, and I made sure that when I spoke to him Matt was there.'

'Ah.' Grace remembered from their college days how manipulative Julia could be when she chose. 'And I suppose he was bowled over by your charm and beauty,' she remarked teasingly. 'How long did it take you to get him to ask you out?'

'Oh, a long time.' Julia dimpled. 'It must have been twenty-four hours, at least. It might have been sooner if we hadn't been staying the night with Maria's sister. As it was, he took my phone number and called the next day.'

Grace arched a silvery brow. 'He must have been keen.'

'He was.' Julia was complacent. 'We've been going out together ever since.' She put down her coffee and stretched luxuriously. 'It's our anniversary next week.'

Grace was surprised. 'You've been going out together for a year?'

'Six *months*,' protested Julia impatiently. 'You don't think I'd be so happy if we'd been going out together for a year without any commitment, do you?'

Grace shrugged. 'People do it. Marriage isn't always the first thing on a person's mind these days.'

'It is if your name's di Falco,' declared Julia grimly, suddenly losing her ready smile. 'You don't think that old harridan of a grandmother would agree to her beloved Matteo setting up house with his girlfriend, do you? Believe me, Grace, it wouldn't happen. She doesn't want any of her great-grandchildren to have someone else's name.'

'Well, I suppose she has a point.' Grace tried to be objective. 'But I do know couples who've lived together and when the children have come along the father has arranged for them to legally take his name—'

'I'm telling you, it wouldn't happen,' insisted Julia doggedly. 'Honestly, Grace, you don't understand the situation here. Well, the situation with the di Falcos, anyway. Apart from any other objections she might have, the old lady is a staunch Roman Catholic. There's just no way she'd countenance her great-granddaughter's father living—"in sin".'

Julia made quotation marks with her fingers around the last two words, and then reached rather clumsily for her coffee. It was obvious that this subject was one with which she wasn't at all happy, but it was only when she spilled some of her coffee onto her sleeve that Grace actually absorbed what else she had said.

'Her—great-granddaughter's father?' she said somewhat blankly. 'Is this some hypothetical offspring, or what?'

'No.' Julia hunched her shoulders grumpily. 'I forgot to tell you: Matt's been married before.'

'And he has a child?'

'Well, she's hardly a child,' muttered Julia unwillingly. 'She's nineteen, I think. I've only met her once. She's at college in Milan.'

Grace was stunned. 'So he's married!'

'No, he's a widower.' Julia was growing increasingly irritable. 'Do you think I'd be wasting my time if he was married to someone else?'

Grace shrugged. That point was moot. She had no wish to remind her friend that she had had a relationship with one of their married tutors in college. But she had the feeling that there was more to this relationship than Julia was telling her. Not least, how his daughter felt about her.

'Well,' she said now, trying to be positive, 'that's not a problem then. And if you and Matteo—Matt—are in love—'

'*If* we are,' said Julia, putting down her coffee again, and Grace wondered what she'd said to resurrect these doubts. 'Okay, I know he cares about me. He wouldn't want to go on seeing me otherwise. But as for us getting married— well, that's a whole different ball game.'

Grace hesitated. 'But it is what you want?'

'Are you kidding?' Julia blew out a breath. 'Of course it's what I want. But that doesn't mean that Matt—well, it doesn't mean that he'd be willing to fight his grandmother for the privilege.'

'And you suspect he might have to?'

'If this weekend was anything to go by, definitely.' Julia snorted. 'I think she made it blatantly clear that I'm not the woman she wants for Matt.'

Grace sighed. 'Because she didn't speak any English?' She shook her head. 'Isn't that a tiny bit negative? Perhaps she was trying to find out how committed you are to becoming an Italian yourself.'

'It wasn't just the fact that she didn't speak any English,' insisted Julia impatiently. 'For God's sake, she hardly spoke to me at all. And she made sure that I was given a room about half a mile away from Matt's apartments. The di Falco villa is huge, you see. I even had a problem finding my way back to the drawing room before dinner.'

'Even so—'

'Even so, nothing.' Julia shook her head. 'She knew very well that I'd expected to share Matt's apartments. I don't know what century she's living in, but she behaved as if our relationship didn't mean a thing.'

Grace sighed. 'You know what old people are like—'

'I know what she's like,' agreed Julia bitterly. 'She'll do anything she can to split us up.'

'You don't know that.'

'Don't I?' Julia regarded her with accusing eyes. 'What if I tell you that I wasn't the only guest at the villa this weekend?'

'Well…'

'It was the first time I'd had the opportunity to visit Matt's home,' went on Julia resentfully. 'I thought it was just going to be a family occasion, but when we arrived all these other people were there.'

'Well,' began Grace again, 'perhaps she thought it would make things easier for you. Did you ask Matteo about it? Perhaps it was his idea.'

'It wasn't.' Julia spoke flatly. 'He knew nothing about it until we got there. But the real sickener was that the old lady had invited this woman, Caterina Vincenzi. A *contessa*, no less, and fairly obviously the woman the *marchesa* would like to see as the next Signora di Falco.'

'Oh, Julia, did she honestly tell you that?'

'She didn't have to.' Julia's lips twisted. 'There must have been more than a dozen guests at dinner yesterday evening and she was the one who was seated beside Matt. I was tucked away at the end of the table with some old uncle. God, he was disgusting! He slobbered all over his food.'

'Julia!'

'He did.' Julia was indignant. But then, when Grace continued to look at her with wide, disbelieving eyes, she gave a shrug. 'Well, he made plenty of noise,' she said defensively. 'You don't know what it was like, Grace. You weren't there.'

'No.'

Grace conceded that point, and as if realising she was becoming far too agitated Julia took a breath. 'I'm sorry,' she muttered. 'It's not your fault that the old witch lives in the past. Anyway—' Julia's eyes glittered '—I intend to drag her—kicking and screaming, if necessary—into the present. We'll see who has the last laugh when I spring my surprise on her.'

Grace stared at her friend. 'Your surprise?' she echoed, wondering why she felt such a sense of apprehension suddenly, and Julia flung herself back against the cushions of the sofa.

'When she finds out I'm having Matt's baby, of course,' she declared triumphantly. 'She won't be able to dismiss me so offhandedly when she discovers I'm having her precious grandson's child.'

CHAPTER THREE

THE phone rang as Grace was going out of the apartment.

She was tempted to leave it. She was fairly sure the call wouldn't be for her, and she'd made arrangements to go to Viareggio that morning. In the last couple of days, she'd become quite familiar with the buses that ran from Portofalco to the other resorts along the coast, and instead of going to the hassle of hiring a car she'd left the driving to someone else.

But the possibility that it could be one of her sisters calling about her mother compelled her to pick up the receiver. 'Hello,' she said, not yet used to using the Italian *ciao*, and then sank down somewhat weakly onto the arm of the sofa when Matteo di Falco's disturbing voice spoke in her ear.

'Miss Horton.' He paused. 'Grace.' Her name had an unfamiliar resonance on his tongue. 'I was hoping I might catch you.'

'Were you?'

Grace knew she didn't sound particularly friendly, but since Julia had dropped her bombshell about the baby she had found it even more difficult to think of Matteo di Falco without a feeling of distaste. She didn't know how he could allow his grandmother to treat Julia so indifferently. But then, he didn't know that in a few short months she was going to have his child.

'Yes.' Clearly, he had no such reservations. 'I am coming to Portofalco this morning and I wondered if you'd allow me to buy you lunch?'

The gall of the man!

Grace was incensed, her own opinion of his sex rein-

28

forced by his behaviour. 'I'm afraid I have other plans,
signore,' she informed him coldly. 'Now, if you'll excuse
me, I have a bus to catch.'

She would happily have put the receiver down there and
then, but his sardonic, *'A bus!'* had her fairly trembling with
indignation.

'Yes, a bus,' she repeated crisply. 'Or *autobus*, if you
will. It's a large motor vehicle with a wheel at each corner
that delivers its passengers to various points along the
coast!'

The breath he sucked in was plainly audible. 'Yes, I
know what an *autobus* is,' he declared tautly, and Grace
had the uneasy feeling that Julia was unlikely to approve
of her insolence. 'In that case, please do not let me detain
you any longer.'

'I won't,' muttered Grace resentfully, but it was under
her breath, and by the time she had thought of a suitable
rejoinder the line had gone dead.

He'd hung up on her, she realised, slamming down her
own receiver with some force, but although she stood there
for several more seconds, justifying what she'd said to herself, she couldn't deny a certain feeling of remorse at her
behaviour. After all, as she'd told herself before, Julia's
affairs were nothing to do with her, and she doubted her
friend would have defended her with such enthusiasm if
their positions had been reversed.

Still, it was too late now to be having second thoughts,
and she could only hope that he wouldn't complain about
her ignorance to Julia. It would be hard to explain why she
felt so strongly about it. It wasn't as if she and Julia were
that close.

Taking a deep breath, she slipped on her sunglasses, collected the bag and hat she'd bought in Livorno the day
before, and left the apartment. She was determined not to
let what had happened spoil her day, and she made a special
point of smiling at the unctuous old caretaker just to prove
to herself that she could be as sociable as anyone else.

The bus to Viareggio was waiting near the ferry terminal and Grace handed over her *carta arancio,* or orange seven-day pass, to be stamped as she climbed aboard. She'd learned that these bus tickets were sold in advance, and she felt a sense of pride at the speed with which she'd adapted to the arrangements. It was true that many of the people who were already on the bus looked like tourists, but there were locals, too, and she had learned to accept their curiosity about her travelling alone without embarrassment. What was new, after all? she reflected wryly. It was her choice, and she was stuck with it.

But, once again, as the bus set away up the winding road that led out of Portofalco, Grace found her thoughts returning to the conversation she had had with Julia just a couple of nights ago. She still found it hard to accept that her friend had been reckless enough to get herself pregnant in the first place, let alone that she believed it would result in Matteo di Falco's asking her to marry him. Somehow Grace doubted that anyone could force the man she knew to do anything he didn't wish to, and she was very much afraid that Julia had placed too much store in the Italians' love of family.

Of course, she could be wrong. But why then had Julia stated that she intended to wait until there was no chance of her having an abortion before confessing what had happened to the man she loved? *If* she loved him. Given his Italian heritage, surely he'd never agree to it anyway. It was a gamble, and Grace hoped her friend would not be too devastated if things didn't work out the way she'd planned.

Yet Grace's doubts persisted, doubts which had not been dispelled by the phone call she had received this morning. Had Julia known he intended to contact her? Had it been done with her approval and support? Or, as Grace suspected, had it been all Matteo di Falco's idea? The man was a perfect jerk, she thought irritably. He obviously hadn't believed that she might turn him down.

She was getting edgy, and that annoyed her even more. She hadn't come to Italy to get involved in Julia's love life, and she forced herself to look out of the window and concentrate on the view. They were high above the ocean now, with a fantastic vista of sea and cliffs stretching away into the distance on either side. Closer to, the scent of myrtle and wild thyme drifted in through the open windows. If the bus had air-conditioning, the driver didn't use it, and Grace decided that she preferred the warm breeze that fanned her face.

Despite its uncertain beginnings, she enjoyed her visit to Viareggio. Unlike Portofalco, it was famous for its beautiful sandy beach, and she walked along the promenade to the pier, before taking refuge from the sun in the palm-shaded Piazza d'Azeglio. Lunch was a spinach and egg-filled pasta to die for, and by the time she boarded the bus back she felt it had been a day well spent.

It wasn't late when the bus deposited her at the terminal. But it had been a fairly strenuous day, and she was unwillingly aware that she was feeling the effects of doing too much, too soon. She wasn't used to the heat, or to so much activity, and the next day she intended to take her own advice and do nothing at all.

Deciding she needed a drink before tackling the walk up to the villa, she entered the nearby *gelateria* and ordered an ice-cream soda. Italian ice cream was so delicious, as she'd discovered the previous day, and served with fresh lemonade it made a really delightful drink.

She took a table in the window instead of sitting outside, glad of the comparative coolness out of the sun. Happily the spreading awning protected the window, and she set her drink down in front of her and sucked greedily at the straw.

And that was when she saw him. He was sitting behind the wheel of a sleek, dark green convertible that was parked across the narrow street, and if it hadn't been so incredible she'd have said he was staring straight at her.

But he couldn't be.

Nevertheless, Grace's eyes went wide with a mixture of confusion and dismay, and she drew back abruptly so that the straw left her mouth. But her lips were still parted, her pink tongue unknowingly provocative as it explored the corners of her mouth. Oh, God, she thought weakly, what was he doing here?

She wished she'd taken any table but this one now. She felt so exposed; so obvious. But the idea of getting up and moving back into the shadows on the off chance that he might have seen her was ludicrous. He didn't intimidate her. Or, if he did, he must never become aware of it.

Dumping her tote bag on the chair beside her, she determinedly clamped both hands about her glass and resumed drinking. The coldness of the drink was invigorating, the chilled condensation on the glass a boon to her moist palms. He'd go away soon, she told herself, deliberately not looking in his direction. He'd said he was coming to Portofalco, and he had. Her seeing him now was just a coincidence. She was tired, that was all. That was why she felt so threatened by his presence.

But he didn't go away. She drank as much of the lemonade as she could before glancing in his direction again, but he was still there. She thought of ordering another soda, but it would have looked odd when there was still some left in the glass she had. She had no choice but to leave the ice-cream parlour. She just wished for once that she could fade into the crowd.

She had crossed the street and started up the steep slope of the Via Cortese when she heard the car behind her. She knew it was his car. The engine was purring gently at the moment, but there was still an underlying deep-throated roar that spoke of the power that was presently being controlled. Much like the man himself, thought Grace, with a reluctant twinge of irony. She doubted he'd appreciated being put down by a foreigner.

She wished she could quicken her step, but apart from anything else the incline didn't encourage reckless gestures like that. Particularly not in her present condition. Besides, however fast she walked, he could always overtake her. So, instead of pretending she hadn't noticed him, she chose a place that was practically smothered with scarlet bougain- villaea, and leaned back against the wall to wait for him.

At least she'd surprised him, she thought as he brought the powerful car to a halt a few yards down from where she was standing. But that didn't prevent an instinctive tightening in her stomach when he opened his door and got out, or suppress the quiver of apprehension she felt as he climbed the hill towards her.

It annoyed her that she should feel any kind of reaction towards him. He was just another man, after all, and she was usually perfectly capable of dealing with them. But, despite the harshness of his dark features, he was undeni- ably sexy, and, although his black jeans and matching tee shirt were quite ordinary, on his lean, muscled body they acquired a sensual appeal.

'So,' he said, propping his hips against the wall beside her. 'Did you need a rest?'

Grace's lips tightened. Beyond his relaxed form she could see the busy waterfront and the blue waters of the bay. She doubted there could be a more perfect spot for a rendezvous, the lengthening shadows redolent with the per- fume of the flowers. But this was not a rendezvous, she thought irritably. It wasn't even a meeting she had ar- ranged.

'Why are you following me?' she asked, determined not to lose the initiative, but whatever advantage she'd thought she had was quickly disposed of.

'You looked tired,' he said lazily, the sidelong glance he gave her spiked with malice. 'Perhaps I felt sorry for you. It's a long walk back to the villa.'

Grace's hand tightened round the strap of her tote bag, her nails digging painfully into her palms. 'How kind,' she said, refusing to let him see that his words had in any way affected her. 'But I'm sure a man of your—importance has better things to do.'

'Straight to the point, as always,' he remarked, pressing his palms down on the warm stones at either side of him. 'Did you enjoy your trip to Viareggio?'

'How did you—?' Grace began to ask the obvious question and then broke off abruptly. He had evidently seen her get off the bus, and if he was familiar with the timetable he would know which bus it was. She took a deep breath. 'Very much, thank you.'

He straightened then, and for a taut moment she thought he was going to touch her. But all he did was push his fingers into the back pockets of his jeans, arching his back reflexively, before turning to face her.

His eyes swept over her, from the top of her bare head— she had stowed her hat in her tote earlier—to the toes of her scuffed trainers and all points in between. Then he said, 'Come on,' when her cheeks were pink and she was intensely conscious of her sunburned knees and the untidiness of her braid. 'Get in the car. I'll give you a lift.'

Grace took a deep breath. 'I don't want a lift.'

'Yes, you do.' He glanced about him dispassionately. 'Come along. I'm parked in a no-waiting area. You wouldn't want me to have to pay a fine, would you?'

Grace tilted her head. 'I couldn't care less,' she answered, and his mouth compressed with impatience.

'What is your problem?' he demanded. 'Did I bruise that fragile ego of yours? It's no sin to admit you need a rest.'

'I didn't need a rest,' said Grace, clenching her teeth, but she could tell by his expression that he didn't believe her. For God's sake, she wished she'd kept on walking. She'd have been almost at the villa by now.

'As you say,' he declared dismissively. 'But I still insist that you get into the car. Now, do you want to do it without my assistance, or would you rather I picked you up and slung you in myself?'

Grace's jaw dropped. No man had ever threatened to

pick her up before. With her height, and not entirely sylph-like form, she had always been too daunting a prospect, and she stared at him as if she didn't believe a word he said.

'It's not necessary,' she said at last, annoyed to find that he had disturbed her. Not in a sexual way, she assured herself, but there was no doubt that he'd made her look at him in a different light.

'But practical,' he pointed out reasonably. His lips twisted. 'Do you want Julia to think that you don't trust me?'

Grace straightened. Of all the things he could have said, that was the one most likely to persuade her to do as he asked. She most definitely did not want Julia to think she didn't trust him. To do so could create a rift between them she feared might never be breached.

'Oh—if you insist,' she muttered ungraciously, and pretended she didn't see the mocking smile that crossed his face. Striding to the car, she jerked open the passenger-side door before he could do so, curling her long legs beneath the dashboard and wishing she'd been wearing anything else but shorts.

He joined her moments later, the gear console providing a welcome barrier between them. But Grace was still uneasily mindful of his nearness and the not unpleasant scent of his clean male sweat. It was infuriating, she thought as he flicked the ignition and the engine came to life again. It wasn't as if she was lacking in experience where men were concerned, yet his sensuality and casual sophistication left her feeling strangely immature.

'I trust you're using a sun-block on these outings,' he remarked as he put the car into gear, and Grace immediately spread her tote bag to cover as much of her burning knees as possible.

'Of course,' she said, although in truth she hadn't put any of the cream on her legs. 'I'm not stupid.'

'But you think I am?'

Grace looked quickly at him and away. 'I didn't say that.'

'You didn't have to.' He shrugged. 'But I have to wonder what Julia has said to you about me for you to have such an unfavourable opinion of me.'

Grace's breath caught in her throat. 'Julia hasn't given me an unfavourable opinion of you.' She swallowed. 'You must know she thinks you're—' She found it difficult to find a suitable word. 'Marvellous!'

'Really?'

'Yes, really.' She looked at him again, convinced now that he was simply baiting her. 'What is it with you, *signore*? I can't believe you're so desperate for compliments that you need to hear them from me.'

His short laugh lacked humour. 'As I said before, you don't believe in pulling your punches, do you, *cara*?' He slowed to accommodate an elderly couple who were crossing the street in front of them and received a wave of acknowledgement in return. 'And if it's not something Julia has said, then I can only assume that you have taken an instant, and inexplicable, dislike to me. Am I right?'

Was he right?

Grace looked down at her bag, smoothing her long fingers over the folds of canvas, trying desperately to find an answer. She could hardly tell him why she'd taken such an aversion to him. Not without betraying Julia's confidence, at any rate, and she couldn't do that, however tempted she might be to explode his myth of superiority.

'I don't know you, *signore*,' she said at last, and earned a slightly disbelieving glance from those deep-set dark eyes. 'I don't,' she insisted, feeling some relief at having found a reasonable explanation. 'And I'm not used to being familiar with men I only know by reputation.'

'By reputation?' He groaned. 'Heaven protect me from women who judge me by my reputation!'

He was laughing at her now, and Grace was overwhelmingly relieved to see the gates of the Villa Modena up ahead. She realised she had no idea how to deal with him, and she was seriously worried that he was having far more of an effect on her than she would have ever dreamed possible. Indeed, she was afraid that half the antagonism she felt towards him stemmed from her own unwilling attraction towards him, and it was obviously wiser for her to ensure that she was never in this position again.

'Anyway,' he said now, his voice deepening to a softness that stroked her tortured nerves, 'we can easily remedy that.'

Remedy what?

For a moment, Grace's mind was blank, but then comprehension dawned. 'I think you're making fun of me,' she said, avoiding a direct answer. 'Oh—' *As if she was surprised!* 'Here we are.'

'Just a minute.' His hand closed round her arm, and although it was the last thing she wanted to do she was forced to turn and look at him.

'I beg your pardon?'

'Grace...' The way he said her name caused the hairs on the back of her neck to prickle in sympathetic response. 'Look, I'm not making fun of you.' He paused. 'It's obvious we've got off on the wrong track—'

'Foot.'

'What?'

'It's foot,' said Grace awkwardly, wishing she'd never interfered. 'People get off on the wrong foot,' she added, her face burning. She shook her head at his expression. 'It's not important.'

'If you say so.' His thumb rubbed distractingly against her sensitive flesh. 'Whatever—you've obviously got the wrong impression of my intentions.' His eyes darkened with disturbing warmth. 'I'd like us to be friends, *no*?'

No!

For a moment, Grace thought she'd said the word out loud, but his face hadn't changed so she knew she hadn't done anything so foolish.

'Um—well, of course,' she began, wondering how she could bring Julia into this without giving him the impression that her friend had warned her off. 'Perhaps when we all get to know one another better—'

'I know Julia very well,' he said flatly. 'And that's not what I mean and you know it. I'd like to think you and I could spend some time together without you treating me like last week's bad news, hmm?' He looked down at where his fingers were caressing her arm and grimaced. 'You've obviously got a poor opinion of my sex, yes? Well, I'd like to try and change that.'

Grace gulped. 'You know nothing about me.'

'Okay.' But she sensed he was only humouring her. Dear God, she wondered, what had Julia been telling him about her? She'd never thought of that. '*Bene*, I suggest we get to know one another, as you say. You can't have a problem with that.'

Couldn't she?

Grace just wanted this conversation to be over, not just for her sake, but for Julia's as well. She wasn't sure what he meant, what he wanted, but as far as she was concerned he was off limits in a big, big way.

'Look, I've got to go,' she said, praying her friend wasn't up in the apartment at this moment gazing down on this scene which would look decidedly suspicious from a distance. 'Thank you for the lift.' She swallowed. 'I was tired. It's been a long day.'

'I would have taken you to Viareggio,' he said softly, and although he hadn't moved Grace could feel his eyes on her mouth like a palpable caress. 'Tell me, have you found the time to visit the monastery of our local martyr, Sant' Emilio di Falco?'

He must know she hadn't, thought Grace crossly. She'd only been here a few days, after all. 'Oh, I've got lots of sightseeing to do yet,' she told him, trying to sound crisply positive. 'And now I really must—'

'Let me take you tomorrow,' he broke in, as she'd half

expected he would. 'Or the day after. It's not the easiest place to get to, but I can assure you it's well worth the visit.'

'I'm sure it is, but I don't know what Julia's got planned for the rest of the week,' declared Grace, barely civilly, and, removing his fingers from her arm, she thrust open the car door.

When she was safely on the pavement outside the Villa Modena, she permitted herself one last salvo. 'I intend to hire a car myself, *signore*. I'm sure it will be easier, in the circumstances.'

She thought he'd let her go then; she expected him to drive away without another word, but she hadn't counted on his innate courtesy. As she waited, hands clutching her tote bag like a lifeline, he vaulted out of the vehicle, coming round to where she was standing rooted to the spot.

'I'll see you to the apartment,' he said, and although she wanted to tell him it wasn't necessary his expression now warned her that she had probably said too much already. So, without another word, she walked rather jerkily through the gates, entering the building through the arched door-way, and ascending the shallow staircase that rose on her right.

She heard rather than saw the old caretaker emerge from his apartment on the ground floor and gaze after them, but she didn't stop to offer a greeting as she normally did. There were two flights of stairs to Julia's apartment, and she climbed them without pausing, only aware that her knees were shaking when she reached the second landing.

It was necessary to find her key when she reached the door, but to her relief it came easily into her hand. Then, pushing it into the lock, she turned to face him, her fingers on the handle behind her supporting her quivering legs.

'Thanks again,' she said, brushing her braid back over her shoulder. 'At least I've got a bit more time to make Julia a meal.' She forced herself to go on. 'Unless she's going out with you, of course. Then I'll only have to cook for one. But, in any case, I'll find the time to tell her how—how kind you've been.'

'Will you?' He didn't sound particularly interested in what she told his girlfriend. 'If you take my advice, you'll forget about running after Julia, and have a bath and then get into bed. We both know you're exhausted. That's why you can't cope with how you feel. But don't insult me by pretending you harbour any gratitude towards me. Our association—short though it is—has progressed much too far for that.'

CHAPTER FOUR

IT WAS the following evening before Grace got a chance to talk to her friend again.

Julia had phoned the previous evening to say that she'd been asked to work an extra couple of hours and that Grace should expect her when she saw her. 'You go to bed if you're tired,' she'd suggested kindly, knowing in advance how Grace had intended to spend her day. 'I'll see you in the morning.'

But in the morning Grace slept late, having spent most of the night fretting about her encounter with Matteo di Falco, and by the time she emerged from her bedroom Julia had gone.

Consequently, it was a good twenty-four hours before she could tell Julia what had happened and by then much of the resentment she had been feeling had dispersed. Perhaps she had overreacted, she brooded. He had only been civil, after all. And time had a habit of making the memory selective so that she was no longer so certain of the facts.

Her doubts weren't helped by Julia's reaction either. The other woman seemed to regard what had happened as characteristic of Matteo. 'He's like that,' she declared carelessly. 'He must have realised how beat you were. I'm sorry if you thought he shouldn't have followed you. I guess he thought he was only being kind.'

Kind was not an adjective Grace would have used to describe Matteo di Falco, but Julia didn't really want to hear about that. And, in the circumstances, there was no way Grace could have told her about his offering to take her to the monastery of Sant' Emilio di Falco. She was

41

afraid if she did so Julia might suspect she was trying to split them up, when in fact that was the last thing she wanted to do.

All the same, she had spent at least part of the previous night worrying whether Julia had any real grounds for believing that, just because she was carrying his child, Matteo would agree to marry her. The more Grace thought about him, the more convinced she became that he was unlikely to be coerced into anything, whatever pressure his grandmother might put upon him. He might deny it, for instance. He might even call Julia a liar. And even if a blood test eventually proved his paternity, who would look after Julia until the baby was born?

Grace found it all very unsatisfactory, and she knew that if she was in Julia's shoes there was no way she'd be able to wait cold-bloodedly for several months before telling Matteo she was pregnant. In fact, she found the whole idea of Julia's being pregnant rather repugnant, and she didn't really approve of the underhanded way she was keeping it to herself.

That was why, when they were sitting on the balcony, having a glass of wine after supper, she felt compelled to bring the subject up again. However reluctant she might be to talk about Matteo di Falco, she told herself she had to try and understand Julia's motives.

'When—when did you find out?' she asked. And then, seeing Julia's blank expression, and realising she wasn't privy to her thoughts, she added hurriedly, 'About the baby? How long have you known?'

Julia shrugged. 'Not long,' she said offhandedly. 'Why do you ask?'

'Well—for obvious reasons,' murmured Grace awkwardly. 'I mean, I just wondered when you intend to tell—Matt.'

Julia cast her a sardonic look. 'I thought I already told you,' she remarked drily. 'When I'm sure the *marchesa* can't do anything about it.'

'But do you really think she'd suggest you have an abortion, anyway?' Grace persisted. 'She does have a Catholic background and I don't think—'

'You'd be surprised,' Julia broke in. 'These old aristocrats will do anything to protect their bloodlines, believe me.'

Grace sighed. 'So when will you feel it's safe to tell them? Two months, three months? *Six* months? How long do you think you can hide it? Babies show!'

'Not all babies,' retorted Julia. 'Actually, I was reading a case the other day of a girl, a teenager, actually, who knew nothing about it until the baby arrived.'

'You're not a teenager, Julia.'

'I know that. But that doesn't mean it couldn't happen to me.' She sipped her wine. 'I don't know why you're asking all these questions.' Her brows drew together in sudden consternation. 'You haven't said anything to Matt?'

'Of course not.' Grace was grateful that she could answer that question without restraint. 'But—well, don't you think you ought to tell him? You're still working full time. He might want you to give up your job.'

'And he might not,' declared Julia flatly, raising one knee and examining a tiny red mark on her skin. 'Dammit, I've been bitten. Let's go back inside.'

Grace left the balcony with some reluctance. The insects didn't bother her, and the night air was soft and seductive. She could smell the night-blooming flowers from the garden below, and somewhere close at hand a violin was playing. She could also hear the sound of laughter and the muted murmur of voices from a party someone was giving further down the street. For the first time in ages, she found herself wishing she was going out this evening. There was something about the atmosphere here, a sense of hedonism and sensuality, that was hard to ignore.

'I think I'll go to bed,' said Julia as Grace entered the living room. She finished the wine in her glass and set it down on the counter in the kitchen with an audible clunk.

Grace was surprised the stem didn't break at such uncaring treatment, but it was evidently stronger than it looked. 'You don't mind, do you? I was fairly late last night.'

Grace shook her head. 'Of course not,' she said, feeling mean for even wishing Julia could change her mind. It wasn't her friend's fault that she'd chosen to spend the whole day in the apartment. She'd reputedly come here to have a rest. She had a good book to entertain her. Perhaps she should have an early night, too.

But, although she'd intended to use the bathroom as soon as Julia was finished, the water stopped running, Julia's door opened and closed, and still Grace lingered in her chair. She was restless—a feeling that was unfamiliar to her, but clearly identifiable. She needed something, anything; the trouble was, she didn't know what.

Getting up, she paced about the living room, stepping out onto the balcony, and resting her bare arms on the wrought-iron balustrade. Breathing deeply, she tried to calm the agitation inside her, but all she succeeded in doing was filling her lungs with the sensuous perfume of the flowers. Perhaps there was something in their scent, she mused wryly, but she couldn't ever remember reading that jasmine or honeysuckle, or even the exotic oleander that grew in scarlet clusters round the crumbling fountain, possessed narcotic properties.

Perhaps she should go for a walk, she considered. It wasn't late, only nine o'clock, and there were still plenty of people about. If she walked down to the harbour, she could always get a taxi back.

The idea took root and flourished. Why not? she asked herself again. She wasn't the nervous type, and she had few fears for her own safety. She would have preferred to go with Julia, but in her absence she could go alone.

Straightening, she glanced down at what she was wearing. The slip dress with its pattern of orange lilies on a purple background was perfectly suitable for what she had planned, but she took a thin silk shawl to cover her shoulders, just in case it was cool down at the quayside. Then, after checking that the French braid she had fastened earlier was still in place, she left the apartment before she could change her mind.

The thick heels of her sandals clattered on the marble stairs as she descended, but she doubted anyone would hear her. It appeared as if Julia's was the only apartment not hosting a social gathering of one sort or another that evening, and the mingled aromas of wine and pasta made Grace's mouth water.

It seemed hours since she and Julia had eaten the cheese and salad that Grace had rustled up after her friend got home. Julia had come in, kicked off her shoes, and sprawled on the sofa with a magazine, and despite her assertion that she didn't expect Grace to cook for her so far she had made no overtures in that direction herself.

Grace had thought Julia might bring something in with her. She'd told her friend she didn't intend to go out today, but her words had evidently fallen on stony ground. In consequence, Grace had had to improvise, and although the meal had been tasty she now felt she knew where she stood. In future, she'd make sure they had plenty of food in the fridge.

Perhaps she'd treat herself to a gooey dessert, she reflected now as the caretaker, who never seemed to miss her comings and goings, emerged from his apartment as she reached the ground floor. Italians traditionally ate later than she was used to, and she wasn't worried that the cafés might be closed.

The caretaker frowned when he saw she was alone. 'Signorina Calloway?' he said, glancing meaningfully up the stairs, and Grace heaved a sigh before miming that she was going out alone.

'Ah, no, signorina.'

The caretaker shook his head, his hands fluttering as he endeavoured to explain what he wanted to say. But his accent was thick enough to cut, and Grace could only guess what he meant.

'I'll be fine,' she said, making a calming gesture, but the old man was not prepared to let her go without a fight.

He said something else, and Grace identified the word *ragazzos* in his anxious protest, which even she knew meant boys. It was obvious he was trying to warn her to be careful, and she felt a reluctant sympathy towards him for his concern.

'No problem,' she insisted. 'I'll get a—a taxi, yes? Back.'

The old man gestured towards his apartment. 'Taxi now?'

'No.' Grace sighed again. 'Really.' She held up her hand. 'I'll be all right, honestly.' She patted his arm. 'Um—thanks, anyway.'

The old man had to let her go, and despite her assertion to the contrary Grace did become slightly nervous walking into town. There were people about, but as the old man had tried to warn her many of them were young men, who stared at her with amorous eyes, and turned to watch her as she hurried by. Some even called after her, making sucking noises with their lips. But she managed to make it appear that she was with someone else at these times, shrinking into the shadows whenever she could.

Rather than run the gauntlet of the crowds along the waterfront, Grace decided to patronise the café she had used the morning after her arrival at the villa, and it wasn't until she was seated at the table and the waiter came to take her order that she realised it was the same young man who had attended to her then as well. Evidently, he had remembered her, too, incredible as that might seem, and she could only assume it was her height that had reminded him she'd been there before.

'Buona sera, signorina. Come stai?'

Acknowledging her elevation to signorina again, Grace

couldn't help a smile. *'Bene, grazie,'* she said, proud of the small grasp of the language she'd made. *'E lei?'*

His delight was obvious. *'Ah, multo bene, signorina,'* he answered swiftly. *'Cosa prende?'*

Grace's tongue circled her upper lip. 'I—' She had no real idea what he meant. 'Um—*un cappuccino, sì?'*

'Un cappuccino?' His teeth were very white between his rather thick lips. *'Bene, signorina. Subito.'*

Grace breathed a sigh of relief when he went to get her order, but he wasn't gone long before he was back. As he bent to set the coffee on the table in front of her, he murmured, *'Bella, signorina,'* and she realised he had assumed she'd come back to see him.

He said something else in a low voice as he tore the slip on which he'd written her order from his pad. Then, seeing her lack of comprehension, he resorted to English, murmuring softly that he would be finished at ten o'clock.

It was almost that already, and Grace forced herself not to panic. But it was difficult to give someone the brush-off when she didn't speak their language, and she had the feeling that he wasn't likely to be co-operative in that department.

'I'm sorry,' she said, looking down at her coffee. 'I think you've made a mistake.' But although she knew he had other customers waiting he didn't go away.

'I see you later, hmm?' he persisted, his hand brushing her shoulder deliberately as he bent to straighten the spoon in her saucer. 'I show you good time, *sì?'*

'No.'

Grace was getting anxious. Without touching her coffee, she pushed back her chair and got to her feet just as another man reached the table. The chair connected with his thigh, and she heard him give a muffled oath. But when she swung round, somewhat guiltily, to apologise she realised why his voice had sounded so familiar.

She shouldn't have been pleased to see him, but she was. In the present circumstances, she'd have welcomed any familiar face. It was only at the back of her mind that she wondered if he had been following her again, and if he had she ought not to be so glad that he was there.

'Is there a problem, *cara*?' Matteo asked, his eyes holding Grace's deliberately, and she realised he knew exactly what had been going on, and was giving her a chance to extricate herself from the situation.

'Oh—you're here,' she said, forcing a tight smile to her lips, and she sensed the waiter's instinctive recoil. 'I—' She glanced about her, aware that they were attracting the attention of other diners. 'Um—are you going to join me?'

'Why not?' With an involuntary rub of his jean-clad thigh, Matteo took hold of the chair and assisted her back into her seat. Then, pulling out a chair opposite, he subsided onto it, glancing up at the waiter with a faintly challenging look. '*Un espresso, pronto, per favore.*'

'*Sì, signore.*'

If the waiter was peeved, he hid it manfully, but Grace was grateful when he walked away. What with the provocation she'd had to put up with on the way down to the harbour and now this, she was justifiably rattled, and it didn't help when Matteo fixed her with a mocking gaze.

'Feeling better?'

Grace thought about picking her coffee up, to give her hands something to do, and then thought better of it. She was aware that she was trembling, and she wasn't totally convinced that she could blame the waiter for that. She was reminded once again of how disturbing the man opposite could be, and although it had been kind of him to come to her rescue she suspected that his motives were not entirely impartial.

'I was just leaving,' she said, deciding not to humour him, and then coloured when his eyes alighted on her cup.

'Without drinking your coffee,' he observed. 'How unusual. Unless it's not to your taste, of course.'

'It's fine.' Grace took a deep breath. 'You know it's

fine.' She paused, and then asked, 'Have you been following me again?'

His lips twitched, and he raised one finger to them. 'Shh,' he murmured teasingly. 'You make me sound as if I'm stalking you.'

'And aren't you?'

She was indignant, but although his expression sobered somewhat he didn't take offence. 'As a matter of fact, my being here is not accidental,' he conceded. 'But before you start calling the *polizia*, I should tell you that old Benito sent me.'

'Benito?' Grace's mind was blank.

'Benito Rossi. At the villa,' said Matteo patiently. 'He was concerned about you coming into town alone.'

'Oh—you mean the caretaker!' exclaimed Grace abruptly, and Matteo inclined his head. 'But—' Her mind raced. 'What were you doing at the villa?'

He shrugged. 'Do I have to answer that question?'

Grace flushed. 'Julia didn't tell me she was expecting you tonight. Besides...' She regarded him warily. 'She couldn't have expected to see you. She's in bed.'

'Perhaps the fact that she is in bed would not be a problem,' he remarked, his eyes mocking, and Grace was unpleasantly reminded of what she knew and he didn't.

'Perhaps not,' she agreed stiffly. 'But all the same I think she'd have warned me if she'd known you were coming.'

The waiter returned at that moment with Matteo's espresso, and he took a couple of bills out of his wallet and paid for both coffees before Grace could object. 'Allow me,' he said when she would have reimbursed him, and she decided it wasn't worth arguing about.

'Okay, Julia did not know of my intention to call at the apartment this evening,' he conceded, when the waiter had departed and they were alone again. He lifted one shoulder in an unconsciously Latin gesture. 'I was going to suggest we might all have dinner together one night this week. Not tonight, obviously, but maybe tomorrow or the day after that.' His dark eyes were an almost tangible invasion. 'I thought it might help to persuade you that I am not the—what shall I say? *Dissipato?*—that you think.'

Grace swallowed. The meaning of the word he had used was obvious enough and she guessed he'd chosen it for that reason. 'I never said you were dissipated, *signore*,' she said, cradling her cup between both palms and lifting it carefully to her lips. So long as her coffee was untouched, she felt compelled to stay here. 'I just don't know why you care what I think of you.'

'Oh, I think you do.' He was sardonic.

'No, I don't.' Her cup clattered into her saucer again. 'And as far as arranging for us all to go out together is concerned, why didn't you just pick up the phone?'

'Good question.' He circled his cup with a lazy finger. 'Perhaps I was hoping that Julia would still be at work.'

Grace gasped. 'You're completely without conscience, aren't you?'

'Am I?' His dark eyes looked straight into hers. 'Why? Because I say what I mean? I can't help it if you've got a problem with that. I guess Julia wasn't exaggerating when she said you had no time for men.'

Grace almost choked. 'Julia said that?'

'Yes. Isn't it true?'

For a moment, Grace couldn't say anything. But then, when she found her voice, it was barely audible. 'I—no.' She shook her head. 'That is—not exactly.'

Matteo arched one dark brow. 'What's that supposed to mean?' he asked, and she found herself explaining.

'I have—men—friends,' she got out jerkily. 'I'm not married, but...nor is she.'

'No.' Matteo conceded the point. 'But I guess the difference is she'd like to be.'

CHAPTER FIVE

WASN'T that the truth?

Grace felt furious suddenly. What was she doing, she wondered, explaining herself to him? Why did she feel the need to defend herself in the first place? It wasn't as if she cared what he thought of her.

'You don't know what I'd like to be,' she said now, and his hand slid across the table to capture hers in a deceptively casual grasp.

'So, tell me,' he prompted huskily, as she marvelled again at how deceitful he was.

'Why?' she demanded now. 'Of what interest could that possibly be to you? When Julia told you I wasn't interested in men, did you decide to try and change my mind, is that it? Do you feel I'm a challenge to your rampant masculinity?'

'So you think my masculinity is rampant,' he observed softly. 'Hmm, that's interesting.'

'No, it's not.' Grace was stung by his mocking ridicule. 'But it's obvious that's what you think of yourself!'

'Do I?' he murmured, his thumb massaging her damp palm. 'And what am I to conclude from the fact that you're trembling? If it's not passion, then you must be angry with me.'

If he only knew...

'I think I'd like to leave,' she said stiffly. 'Please let go of my hand.'

'What? And have you throw back your chair and almost unman some other poor *bastardo*? I do not think the proprietor would thank me for that.'

'I didn't—' Grace's eyes dropped almost compulsively

51

to where his opened jacket exposed the silver buckle of his belt. 'I didn't hurt you.' And then, almost pathetically, she thought afterwards, she asked, 'Did I?'

'And if you did?' His eyes tormented her. 'In your opinion, you've done a service for all the women of Portofalco. Just think of their relief when they discover I've lost my— charm.'

Grace was sure the women of Portofalco would be unlikely to thank her in that instance, but she was equally sure that the situation wouldn't arise.

She held up her head. 'You love making fun of me, don't you?'

'Is that what I'm doing?'

'I think so. Yes.'

'You don't think you are taking what I say a little too seriously?' His voice softened. '*Bene*, you didn't hurt me— well, only a little, all right?'

'You like being provocative, don't you?'

'What? By assuring you that you didn't hurt me before?' His mouth grew sensual. 'If I'd asked you to kiss it better, that would have been provocative, *no*?'

'You're disgusting!' Grace took a deep breath. 'I want to go.'

'But we are just getting to know one another.'

Grace shook her head. 'I can't believe you said that.'

'Why not? What have I said?' He covered her resisting fingers with his other hand and brought the thumb that had been caressing her palm to his mouth. He held her gaze as he sucked the moisture from it, and Grace wanted to die of embarrassment. 'I do want to get to know you. What's wrong with that?'

He had to know. Grace's teeth were clenched with the effort of remaining calm in such trying circumstances. The trouble was, despite what had happened when she was younger, she'd had little real experience with men in recent years. She tended to avoid awkward situations, and she feared she'd become rusty when it came to dealing with the opposite sex.

'And what about Julia?' she demanded now, forced to bring her friend's name back into the conversation. 'You must know that she—' She had to go carefully here. 'You must know she—cares about you.'

'Does she?'

His indifference appalled her. 'Of course she does.'

His nostrils flared with unconscious hauteur. 'Julia has her own agenda, I'll give you that.'

Grace's eyes widened. 'Are you saying you don't care what she thinks of you?' she exclaimed hotly, and then drew back when he leaned towards her across the table.

'I don't think you and I should waste our time talking about Julia,' he said, stroking the backs of her fingers. His mouth compressed for a moment, but then he seemed to dismiss whatever it was that had soured his mood. 'Tell me about yourself,' he urged. 'Tell me about the museum. Yes, I know where you work, but I'm told that you've been ill—'

'Never mind about me,' cried Grace unsteadily. She took another breath, a calming one, she hoped. 'Why don't you tell me about Julia? About the relationship you've been having with her for the past six months? About how close you've become? So close in fact that you invited her to your home to meet your family last weekend—'

Abruptly, she was free. With a curt exclamation in his own language, which Grace was sure wasn't at all complimentary, he flung himself back in his chair and stared grimly around the café. She soon realised he was looking anywhere but at her, and the desire she'd had to rush away wilted in the chill of his obvious contempt.

'I'm sorry if you don't think it's any of my business,' she began lamely, the uneasy silence forcing her to say something in her own defence, and he cast her a scornful look.

'She told you that, did she?' he asked distantly. 'She told

you I'd invited her to Valle di Falco? That I was eager to introduce her to my family?'

'Yes.' But Grace could feel her confidence waning as she tried to remember exactly what Julia had said. 'At least—' She made a concerted effort to speak honestly. 'I suppose I could have assumed that's what she meant.'

Matteo looked at her again, his dark eyes narrowed and intent. 'So if I tell you I did not invite her to the Villa di Falco to meet my family, you'll believe me?'

Grace was confused. 'But she did stay at the villa, didn't she?'

'At the villa, yes.' Matteo blew out a breath. 'She expressed an interest in the vineyard, and I agreed that the next weekend she had free she should come out and see our operation. Unfortunately, Julia took that to mean that I was inviting her for the weekend, and you obviously know the rest.'

Grace frowned. Despite the fact that she didn't want to believe him, what he was saying did have an unholy ring of truth. 'Nevertheless,' she said, forcing herself to go on, 'you must have suspected how she would take it. You have been seeing one another for several months.'

'If you say it's six months, I must accept it,' he said, spreading his hands. 'But please don't run way with the idea that Julia doesn't understand our situation. We've had fun together, yes, but that's all. I think she knows the time has come to move on.'

'To move on?'

Grace's voice had risen alarmingly, and he regarded her with cool, narrowed eyes. 'Why not?' he asked. 'There was no commitment, and she knew it. I have no intention of getting married again.'

Grace's throat was tight. 'But—but you were lovers,' she protested, and lines appeared to bracket Matteo's mouth.

'We slept together,' he corrected her flatly. 'This is not a lifetime's commitment.'

'But you said yourself that Julia would like to be married,' Grace pointed out swiftly, wondering if she was doing her friend any favours by bringing it up.

'Not to me,' declared Matteo, with depressing certainty. 'Now…' He indicated her cup. 'Drink up your coffee and I will take you home.'

Grace pushed back her chair. 'That won't be necessary.'

'Oh, please…' Matteo sounded weary. 'Let us not get into that again.' He, too, got to his feet and came round the table to join her. 'Now, unless you wish to cause another scene, shall we leave without discussing this any further?'

Grace walked ahead of him out of the café, turning when they emerged onto the street to give him a guarded look. 'I should warn you,' she said, 'I don't sleep around.'

His lips tightened. 'Nor do I,' he said, gesturing to where his car was parked on the quay. Then, when she still looked mutinous, he added heavily, 'Grace, I am not your enemy. Now, do me the courtesy of letting me see you home.'

She went with him because it was easier not to argue with him. Or, at least, that was what she told herself. And, after all, she had no desire to run the gamut of the young males she'd encountered on her way down here as she looked for a taxi, or to attract unwelcome attention by having a car tailing her all the way back to the apartment.

Nevertheless, she felt a sense of impotence as he folded his lean frame into the seat beside hers. She didn't want to be with him, she told herself, even as her eyes sought and reluctantly admired the powerful thighs that took control of the expensive car.

He put his right arm along the back of her seat as he turned to reverse the vehicle out of its bay, and her spine stiffened almost instinctively at the nearness of his heated flesh. Her pulse, heightened by her unwilling reaction to him, beat madly in her ears as she turned away. She knew she'd never met a man who affected her so much physically before, and she wondered if she'd been fooling herself all these years by imagining that she was immune to her sexual needs.

The one-way system of roads around the harbour meant he had to drive to the end of the quay before he could turn back towards the Via Cortese, and Grace sat stiffly beside him, wishing she had never left the villa. Apart from the very real anxiety she felt at the prospect of telling Julia she'd seen him, she was now in possession of facts that she really didn't want to know.

'What are you thinking?' Matteo asked, slowing at an intersection, and Grace wondered if it would do any good to tell him how she felt.

'That Julia will probably kill you when she finds out you followed me into town,' she said, not altogether truthfully. In actual fact, Julia was more likely to want to kill *her*! She cast a helpless look in his direction. 'Don't you care what she thinks at all?'

'*Dio mio!*' Matteo groaned. 'I thought we had dealt with my relationship with Julia. She may be jealous, yes. But, believe me, Julia does not care about me.'

Grace swallowed the retort that sprang to her lips. She wanted to say, She does. She wanted to say, She's going to have your baby, and she expects you to marry her. But she couldn't. It wasn't up to her. It wasn't even her problem. Yet she suspected it wasn't going to be that simple, and that, for all her inhibitions, she *was* involved, whether she liked it or not.

'Did you get a car?' he asked as they reached the villa, and Grace, who had been caught up in the confusion of her thoughts, gazed at him with uncomprehending eyes. 'You said you were going to hire a car,' he reminded her, and she realised that as far as he was concerned nothing had changed. What was more, his expression was disturbingly tender, arousing emotions that Grace knew she had no right to feel.

'I—' She forced herself to concentrate on what he was saying. 'Um—no, not yet. There hasn't been time. I didn't go out today,' she added, aware that she was being far too generous in the circumstances. 'After yesterday, I decided I needed some time to rest.'

'After the conversation we had?' he asked her mockingly, and to her dismay he cupped her cheek with his hand. His thumb scraped gently over the faint shadows beneath her eye. 'Oh, Grace,' he breathed softly, 'what am I going to do with you?'

'Let me go, I hope,' retorted Grace sharply, but even to her own ears the words sounded brittle. When he bent his head towards her, it wasn't totally unexpected, and when she felt his tongue brush across her lips her heart leapt painfully into her throat.

He couldn't do this, she told herself. He couldn't hold her and kiss her when the woman to whom he owed his affection and his allegiance was upstairs in the apartment nurturing his child in her womb. And what kind of a friend was she for allowing it to happen? She had never had any time for men like him, so why was she letting him touch her now?

The questions were easy enough, the answers rather harder to find. Both of his hands were cradling her face now, holding her still while his mouth moved back and forth against hers. His eyes were open, staring into hers, and although it was too dark to see their expression she could guess what he was thinking.

'Sweet,' he murmured huskily, and then, more hoarsely, *'Cara; dolce amore,'* and Grace felt her senses reeling as those feather-light caresses gave way to an urgent possession.

She gave in, if only briefly. For a fraction of a second, she couldn't prevent herself from responding to the sensual addiction of his mouth. Its heat, its hunger, its conscience-numbing assault was so intensely pleasurable that she couldn't resist, and she found herself craving its almost carnal sexuality long after she'd jerked away.

That she did actually put an end to it was her only redeeming feature, she thought afterwards. It was the only thing she could point to as distinguishing her actions from his. And it wasn't easy. Apart from the fact that Matteo didn't want to let her go, the blood was pounding so madly through her veins, she could hardly hear herself think. Emotions she had long thought aborted were stirring dangerously, and the impulse to indulge them was an inevitable temptation.

But somehow she managed to retain a small shred of sanity, so that when he resisted her withdrawal she was able to find the strength to drag herself away. With an almost animal sound of anguish, she thrust open the door beside her and jackknifed out of the car, nearly turning her ankle in a grating as she stumbled towards the gate.

It was hardly an elegant retreat. Almost tripping up the steps into the garden of the villa, she expected every moment to feel his hand reach for her arm or hear his angry voice in her ear.

But she didn't. He didn't even follow her, angry or otherwise, and by the time she reached the arched doorway the roar of the powerful engine was just an echo in her ears. Oh, God, he was gone, she thought, and what the hell was she going to do now? No matter how much she might want to, she couldn't tell Julia what had happened. Not in her condition. She was in an impossible situation, and she had no one to blame but herself.

Things didn't look much brighter the next morning.

Despite the fact that exhaustion had claimed her for most of the night, Grace awoke feeling heavy-eyed and weary. Even the relief she felt at discovering that Julia had already left for work seemed treacherous. Sooner or later, she would have to face her. The trouble was, she didn't know what she was going to say.

Perhaps it would be easier all round if she went back to England, she mused unhappily. All right, Julia was bound to wonder why she'd suddenly decided to leave, but better that than have her discover what had happened the night before. And, remembering that conversation, Grace felt doubly depressed. She was sure now that Julia was deluding herself in believing she could manipulate Matteo di Falco into taking responsibility for his child, let alone force him to marry her when he so obviously intended to remain single.

Still, whatever decision she made, they needed to eat, and, determining not to let Matteo di Falco intimidate her, Grace dressed in shorts and a sleeveless polo shirt and left the apartment. There was a *salumeria* or delicatessen just around the corner, and she was sure she could get everything she needed there.

It was a little daunting leaving the villa, particularly as the caretaker hailed her as she was starting down the path. For one awful moment, she thought Matteo had been lying in wait for her, and her palms were moist as she turned round. But the old man only waved and shouted, *'Buongiorno, signorina!'* and she swallowed to ease the sudden dryness in her throat as she returned his greeting.

The phone was ringing when she got back to the apartment. She'd closed the door and started across the room to answer it before she paused to wonder who it might be. It could be Julia, she supposed, but surely her friend would assume she'd be out at this time of day. Grace had been talking of visiting Pisa the night before—before that disastrous foray into Portofalco.

It might be one of her sisters, of course. It was a couple of days since she'd rung to check up on her mother, but she couldn't imagine Pauline or Karen calling at this time of day when the charges were highest.

Which only left Matteo di Falco, and she had no desire to speak to him. After last night's little episode, she had hoped not to have to speak to him again, and the idea that he might still be trying to pursue that sordid little affair filled her with a mixture of frustration and disgust.

Dumping her bags of shopping on the counter in the

kitchen, she began unloading their contents into the fridge. She'd bought veal, and some of the delicious Parma ham that was produced locally, as well as vegetables and cheese, and the makings of a salad, which she'd planned to have for lunch. To her relief, the phone stopped ringing long before she was finished, and as soon as the bread was stowed in its earthenware container she walked out onto the balcony.

The sun was almost overhead, the wrought-iron railing hot beneath her slim fingers. She'd half expected to see the dark green convertible parked in the street beyond the walled garden of the villa, but there were no vehicles in the immediate vicinity. Not that that meant anything, she assured herself. He could have called from anywhere.

She sighed. While she'd been out, she'd almost managed to convince herself that she was exaggerating what had happened the night before. He'd only kissed her, for God's sake! He hadn't attempted to have sex with her or anything, and the things he'd said about his relationship with Julia could have been said to impress her. It didn't say much for his fidelity, of course, but that wasn't her problem, and if Julia was prepared to risk her future with a man like him that was her decision.

But now Grace was on edge again. That phone call had proved how accessible she remained by staying here, and although she hadn't answered it she couldn't go on ignoring every call that came to the apartment. Or could she? Her lips twisted. One way or the other, she had to decide before Julia came home.

She spent the afternoon reading. She'd brought several novels with her, and although up to now she hadn't felt much like reading them today she felt the need for the escapism they offered.

She was half asleep on the bamboo lounger on the balcony when Julia got home, and she blinked up at her friend in some confusion. 'Is it that time already?' she exclaimed, swinging her legs to the floor, and Julia shook her head at her as she subsided onto the other chair.

'Relax,' she said. 'It's only half-past four.' But Grace could see that she was anything but relaxed. There was a kind of suppressed excitement about her friend that did little to calm her own nerves, and she realised she still hadn't decided what she was going to do. 'I didn't think you'd be home yet. Didn't you go to Pisa?'

'Oh—no.' Grace hoped Julia would put the sudden heightening of colour in her cheeks down to the sun. 'I didn't go out. Well, only briefly, anyway. It—it was too hot.'

Julia frowned. 'You didn't go out?'

'Just—shopping—'

'But I rang at lunchtime and you didn't answer.'

'Was that you?' Grace's relief was tempered with impatience. She should have answered the phone. 'It was ringing as I came back in, but—'

'But you didn't get to it in time. I know,' Julia said. 'Well—' Now that earlier air of excitement surfaced again in the way she wrapped her arms about her midriff and hugged herself tightly. 'I have something to tell you. Something fantastic! Guess what? Matt's asked us both to Valle di Falco for the weekend!'

No!

Grace was horrified. 'You mean—to the Villa di Falco?' she asked faintly, so that Julia wouldn't notice how shocked she must look. But her mind was racing with the knowledge that once again he had outmanoeuvred her.

'Yes, to the villa,' agreed Julia, too engrossed with her own feelings to notice how her friend might be taking this. 'I was sure I'd blown it last weekend, what with the old lady being so standoffish and everything, but Matt said that I had overreacted and that the *marchesa* was looking forward to seeing us.' She cast a mischievous glance in Grace's direction. 'Both of us, can you believe it? Maybe I've got you to thank for the invitation.'

Grace gasped. 'Oh, I don't think—'

'Nor do I, silly!' exclaimed Julia impatiently. 'I was only teasing. Obviously, they've included you because they know you're my guest. That's all.'

'Then I won't go.'

'No, you must.' Julia stared at her imploringly now. 'I mean it, Grace. The invitation's for us both, and the last thing I want to do is offend the old lady again.'

Grace made a helpless gesture, any plans she might have had of leaving vanquished by the look on her friend's face. But she was painfully aware of her own inexperience, nonetheless. To think she'd been worrying about him waiting for her outside the villa or pestering her with phone calls. How naïve she'd been. Instead of doing something she might have stood a chance of thwarting, he'd completely blindsided her, and short of telling Julia exactly what she thought of him and his invitation she was stuck. He was so damned arrogant, she thought bitterly. He must be very confident that she wouldn't tell Julia what he'd done. She wished desperately that Julia wasn't pregnant so that she could do just that.

'You will come, won't you?' Julia was pleading now. 'You'll enjoy it. It's a beautiful place; a fabulous house. And you never know, you may be able to put in a good word for me with the *marchesa*.'

Grace stifled a groan. 'Oh, Julia...'

'I'll take that as a yes,' declared her friend triumphantly. 'Oh, I can't wait! A whole weekend with Matt. What a marvellous opportunity!'

For whom? brooded Grace dully, wondering if she could possibly be wrong. Was she being as insufferably arrogant as he was in thinking that this whole scheme had been engineered for her benefit? She felt her nails digging into her palms. One way or another, she was going to find out.

CHAPTER SIX

IF GRACE had hoped—*dreaded*?—that she might find out before they left for Valle di Falco, she was disappointed. She had no way of contacting Matteo, even if she'd wanted to, and in the time that remained before they were to leave for the di Falcos' villa she was kept busy doing chores for Julia.

To begin with, Julia apparently employed no housekeeper, and the whole apartment needed a thorough cleaning by the end of the week. Plus, there were all the little errands that Julia expected her to run for her. It seemed her friend was always in need of something from the *farmacia* in the town, and if it hadn't sounded so paranoid Grace might have wondered whether Julia wasn't deliberately inventing things for her to do so she wouldn't have time to think about changing her mind.

She'd phoned home again, half hoping that her sisters were finding it difficult coping with their mother. But it seemed they were managing quite happily, which made Grace wonder why they hadn't offered to help out before. She guessed the truth was that she had always been available, and without any family ties of her own they'd probably assumed she was glad of her mother's company.

And she was, mostly. It hadn't been easy, of course, and when holidays had come around she would have welcomed some support. Her mother, she knew, was desperate not to be a burden to anybody, so Grace had always tried to avoid any arguments on her account.

On Thursday evening, Julia told her that Matteo was sending a car to pick them up the following afternoon. 'I'll be finishing work at lunchtime,' she added. 'I've got some extra hours due to me with working last weekend, so I should be home by two o'clock. Is that all right?'

Grace's mouth compressed. 'If I must go,' she said, aware that her attitude could be misconstrued as sour grapes. She paused. 'I'm surprised he's not coming for you himself.'

'For *us*,' Julia corrected her impatiently. 'And we couldn't all fit into his Lamborghini, could we?' She grimaced. 'I hope you're not going to spoil the weekend, Grace. I'd have thought that as a historian yourself you'd have been interested in Italian art and architecture.'

'I am, of course—'

'There you are, then.'

'It's just—well, I'm sure I'm going to be in the way.'

'Not a bit of it.' Julia was vehement. 'I'm hoping you'll keep the old lady off our backs. You know what they say about three being a crowd.'

Grace's lips twitched in reluctant response, but the more she heard about Julia's plans for the weekend, the more apprehensive she became. She couldn't imagine Matteo's grandmother welcoming two Englishwomen into her home when she'd objected to one. She was sure the next three days were going to be a disaster, and nothing Julia could say would reassure her.

The car that arrived to take them to the villa was a vintage Rolls-Royce. Grace didn't know what kind of car Julia had expected, but judging by her expression this wasn't it. But for her part Grace was absolutely enchanted by its gleaming chassis and famous insignia. Inside, it gleamed just as brightly, with shiny leather seats and polished wood.

'As if he couldn't have sent the Mercedes,' Julia grumbled as the uniformed chauffeur stowed their cases in the capacious boot. 'It doesn't even have seatbelts,' she added as Grace joined her on the spacious rear seat. 'And the suspension probably leaves a lot to be desired, too.'

'Stop moaning,' said Grace, her own spirits unaccountably heightened by the sight of the old car. 'This thing is probably worth twice as much as the Mercedes. It's a museum piece, Julia. I think we're privileged to ride in it.'

'Are you sure?' Julia stared at her. 'You think it's worth twice as much as a Merc?'

'I don't know.' Grace wished she'd never made that comparison now. It sounded mercenary. 'I just meant it's a really beautiful vehicle.'

'Mmm.'

Julia's scarlet-tipped fingers caressed the smooth leather of the armrest, and Grace could practically see the calculation in her face. It made her wonder about Julia's real motives for wanting to marry Matteo di Falco. Did she love him? Or had her reasons for getting pregnant more to do with what he had to offer in other ways?

It wasn't something Grace wanted to even think about. Particularly not right now. The fact was, Julia was pregnant, and one way or another Matteo was going to have to pay. Whether Julia was right and he would agree to fulfil his responsibilities to her was not a situation she wanted to contemplate. The alternative was just as repugnant in her eyes.

The journey to Valle di Falco took them away from the coastal strip and into the hills that surrounded the small port. And once off the coastal highway the road became much narrower and much more hazardous, winding its way around a series of hairpin bends with only a flimsy guardrail between them and the precipitous drop below. It was quite daunting looking down on the tops of swaying firs and cypress trees, but the smell of fresh pine was quite heady, with yellow broom and clumps of wild roses providing vivid slashes of colour.

Now and then, they glimpsed the roofs of isolated dwellings, perched on the side of hills that were lushly spread with vegetation. Here and there, villages nestled in the valleys, and the tinkling notes of cowbells drifted on the afternoon air. Once they heard the distinctive toll of a monastery bell, and Grace wondered if it was the same monastery that Matteo had spoken about. Then she chided herself for even thinking of him. She distrusted everything about him, particularly the way he had manipulated her into seeing him again.

It was late afternoon when they neared their destination and long shadows lay over the curving descent into the valley below. Grace caught her breath as a flock of goats was herded across the road in front of them, without any apparent regard for their safety, and the chauffeur leaned out of the window and indulged in a brief, but fiery, exchange with their keeper.

'Goodness, I thought we were going to run them down,' she murmured in an undertone as the car accelerated past, but her friend wasn't listening to her. Instead, she was staring eagerly out of the window, and Grace's nerves tightened again when Julia clutched her arm.

'Look!' she exclaimed, apparently unconcerned about the well-being of a flock of goats. She pointed a finger. 'There: can you see it? On that rise at the far side of the valley. That's the villa.' She licked her lips in obvious anticipation. 'Isn't it a fantastic sight?'

Grace forced herself to make some suitable comment, but the sprawling roofs of the collection of buildings she could see only filled her with a sense of apprehension. The castle-like towers and cupolas that were visible above a protective screen of dark green cypress trees hinted at the fact that the Villa di Falco was far more imposing than even she had imagined, and she pressed her palms together in her lap.

'Of course, the vineyards are interesting, too,' Julia continued, indicating the unmistakable rows of vines that grew on the terraced slopes and over the valley floor. 'Did you know that black grapes can be used to make white wine as well as red? It's the flesh under the skin that's important. Matt told me that last weekend.'

Grace tried to show some interest, but in all honesty she didn't care what grapes the di Falcos grew. She wasn't here to get a crash-course in viticulture. She had still to face his grandmother, which was something she was not looking forward to, and she prayed that when she saw Matteo again she would be able to hide her animosity from Julia.

As well as the grapes, Grace saw groves of olive trees as they drove towards the villa. Hamlets, too, and farmhouses were dotted about the valley, some of them probably providing homes for the estate workers, she assumed. The inviting sound of a small waterfall tumbling down the hillside indicated the presence of running water, and as they reached the avenue of tall poplars that marked the approach to the villa she glimpsed the lake that lay in quiet splendour in front of its gates.

An hour later, Grace was sitting at an enormous satinwood dressing table, attempting to restore some colour to her unnaturally pale cheeks. She'd developed quite a headache, due no doubt to the fact that they hadn't met their host and hostess yet. According to the black-clad housekeeper who had admitted them, the *marchesa* was resting and would join them for drinks before dinner, while Signor Matteo had been unexpectedly called away to Siena, and offered his apologies for not being there to greet them on their arrival.

Not unnaturally, Julia hadn't been at all suited at this news. Fortunately, her grasp of the language was much greater than Grace's, and she'd conveyed what the housekeeper had said to her friend. Nevertheless, her attitude had been somewhat less than gracious, and it was partially due to her rudeness that Grace had a headache now.

For her part, Grace was grateful for any time spent without the stress of Matteo di Falco's presence, even if Julia had made their arrival something of an ordeal. And the fact that they were to be accommodated in the east wing of the villa, which Julia declared irritably was where she had stayed before, meant there was a satisfying distance between them.

'I really thought Matt would have ignored his grand-

mother this time,' Julia added as a uniformed maid escorted
them along a cool, echoing corridor whose tiled floor reminded Grace of something she'd previously only seen in
the museum. 'I'm sure you wouldn't have minded if we
hadn't been together, would you? Oh, I'll just have to try
and persuade him to move me later.'

Their apartments—Grace felt she could hardly call them
rooms—were equally magnificent. In other circumstances,
Grace knew she would have been fascinated by her surroundings. But Julia's resentment was all-pervading, and
she'd managed to dispel what little enthusiasm Grace had.

Nevertheless, she couldn't help but admire the villa's
elegance. They had each been given a suite of rooms, com-
prising a bedroom, a dressing room, and an adjoining parlour, and although the furniture was of stately proportions
it was dwarfed by the rooms themselves. In the bedroom,
where she was now, the embossed, linen-covered walls
reached up to a ceiling which must have been at least
twenty feet above her head. Alabaster nymphs and cherubs
frolicked around the cornice, while the embroidered canopy
of the tester bed drew attention to the bunches of grapes
and other exotic fruits carved on its posts.

A marble-topped washstand, also elaborately carved, was
set with a porcelain jug and basin, which Grace guessed
must once have provided the only means of taking a wash.
But now one of the adjoining apartments had been con-
verted into a bathroom, with a half-sunken tub that was
almost big enough to take a swim in.

A couple of comfortable armchairs and a table, plus various chests of drawers, made up the rest of the furnishings
in the room, while the dressing room next door contained
a pair of matching armoires, which had swallowed up the
few clothes Grace had brought with her.

It was living on the grand scale, she reflected, and not
something she was used to. But it helped to explain
Matteo's attitude, she thought reluctantly. It would be hard
to be brought up in these surroundings without acquiring a

certain arrogance, and she wondered if Julia would really be happy here.

She was in the parlour, fastening a pair of gold studs to her earlobes, when someone knocked at the door.

'Come in. It's open,' she called, expecting it to be Julia, and then turned in dismay when Matteo di Falco came into the room.

'Hi,' he said, closing the door behind him, seemingly immune to her hostility. 'I just came to see if you have everything you need.'

Grace abandoned her attempt to insert the second stud and regarded him coldly. 'I had everything I needed at the apartment,' she said, aware that she was trembling. 'Julia will be here any minute. I think you'd better go.'

'Julia's not ready yet. I checked,' he replied dispassionately, surveying her with enigmatic eyes. 'Are you?'

Grace didn't know how to take that. Not expecting to be attending any formal occasions, she hadn't brought many clothes to Italy with her. Her ankle-length black sheath, with its knee-high slits at either side, was not an evening dress, and she could have worn it equally well to go into town.

'As I'll ever be,' she declared, annoyed that his words should affect her. 'I'm sorry if you don't think I look smart enough to meet your grandmother.'

'Did I say I didn't like what you were wearing?' In navy blue trousers and a matching silk jacket, no one could have accused Matteo of being underdressed, and her lips tightened at the realisation that she was assessing his appearance, too. His brows lifted. 'As always, you look beautiful.' His voice thickened. 'Very beautiful.'

'Oh, yeah, right.'

Grace tried to sound as sardonic as her words but the look in his dark eyes was obsessive, and she could feel its magnetism piercing her flesh and spreading out through her body like some mind-numbing drug.

To escape its consequences, she swung away, groping

for the gold stud and trying desperately to slip it into her ear. But her hands were slippery with sweat and she dropped it, and it was Matteo himself who rescued the small fob from the woven rug beneath their feet.

'Let me,' he said huskily, and because Grace knew she hadn't a hope in hell of doing it herself she turned obediently and presented her ear to him.

She'd acted on impulse, without giving a thought to how she would feel when his cool fingers brushed her neck, and the unintentional intimacy it evoked caused the pulse behind her ear to palpitate alarmingly. His breath, warm and lightly tinged with the toothpaste he had used, fanned her heated skin, turning what she'd thought of as a convenience into a wholly sensual encounter.

'Do I make you that nervous?' he asked softly, and because his fingers were still touching her neck she couldn't be sure whether he was finished or not.

'I don't know what you—' she began, only to have him stroke the fluttering pulse with his thumb.

'Calm down,' he said mildly. 'I'm hardly likely to make love to you here—'

'As if I'd let you,' she said in a hoarse voice, but when she tried to move away his hand descended on her neck with rather more force.

'Do you want me to prove it?' he demanded, the glitter in his eyes warning her that she was not dealing with an impassive Englishman here. The fingers of his free hand touched her lips. 'It wouldn't be difficult, believe me.'

Grace's eyes were wide. 'Aren't you making a mistake here?' she asked tremulously. 'It's Julia you should be saying these things to, Julia who thinks you've invited her here again to make amends for what happened last weekend.'

'But we know differently, don't we?' he inserted smoothly, and this time when he bent his head she felt his teeth against the skin of her neck. 'It would be so easy,' he muttered. 'But I won't do it.'

'Do what?'

She had steeled herself against any attempt he might have made to draw her against his lean, muscled frame, but she was not prepared for the seductive appeal of his words.

'Mark you,' he said regretfully, lifting his head. 'I think my grandmother might find that a rather primitive way of staking my claim.' His eyes dropped to where her breasts betrayed her agitation. 'I'll have to think of another way.'

'As you did with Julia?' demanded Grace stiffly, and with a muffled oath his hands dropped to his sides and he stepped away from her.

'Okay,' he said, pushing his hands into the pockets of his jacket. 'I should have known it was a bad idea bringing Julia here again, but I couldn't think of any other way I could get you to agree to come—'

'You got that right!'

'So I shall have to think of a way to dispose of the problem she presents,' he continued flatly. 'But—for the moment—I suppose I deserve your condemnation.'

Grace stared at him. 'You don't get it, do you?' she exclaimed. 'I don't care what you do with Julia. I don't care whether she's here or not. I don't want to have anything more to do with you.'

'Oh, right.' He regarded her sceptically. 'That's why you practically go to pieces every time I touch you. Think again, *cara*. You want to make love with me, every bit as much as I want to make love with you.'

'No!'

'Yes.' He stepped towards her again and took hold of the thick braid that as usual lay over her shoulder. He tugged on it until she tilted her head and his darkening eyes mirrored his satisfaction at the awareness he could see in her face. 'I can't wait to loosen your hair,' he told her harshly. 'I want to thread my fingers through every strand and spread it out around your head on my pillow. Yes, *my* pillow, *cara*. Not yours. I want you in my arms, in my bed, with your silken limbs bared for me and me alone, and nothing and no one is going to stop me.'

Grace couldn't speak. In truth, she could hardly breathe. His words had painted an indelible picture on her subconscious, and although he let her pull away from him she knew he was much cleverer than even she had imagined. Goodness, he didn't need to seduce her; he didn't even need to touch her. The connection he had so effortlessly created between them was far stronger than any physical bond, and she felt dizzy with the power he was exerting over her.

'I want you to leave; now,' she choked, and with a careless shrug of his shoulders he sauntered towards the door.

'I'll send Gina to show you the way to the *loggia*,' he remarked, pausing in the doorway. Then, with one of those devastating changes of mood, his eyes gentled. 'Don't look at me like that, *cara*,' he advised her softly. His lips twisted. 'Especially not when Nonna is watching us, *capisce*? I wouldn't want her to get the wrong idea.'

Grace quivered. 'Could she?'

'Perhaps not.' He conceded the point with a mocking inclination of his head. 'Ceci, then. She's much younger.'

CHAPTER SEVEN

By the time Julia appeared, accompanied by the young maid who was to escort them, Grace had succeeded in regaining a little of her composure. She was still edgy, of course, but she knew Julia would assume that was because she didn't want to be here. And she didn't, she thought despairingly. More than ever now.

'This is Gina.' Julia introduced the maid with careless arrogance, and Grace had to bite back the words, *I know.* 'Apparently Matt has sent her to show us the way to the drawing room.'

'The—drawing room?' Once again, Grace almost betrayed herself, and Julia gave her an impatient look.

'Yes, the drawing room,' she repeated, with mild irritation. 'What's wrong? Are you afraid you're not going to look sophisticated enough for their friends?' Her lips twisted. 'Don't worry. Matt has assured me that we're his grandmother's only guests tonight.'

'I see.' Grace had the feeling there would have been more safety in numbers. 'Um—don't you think this dress is suitable?'

Julia, who was wearing a layered chiffon gown whose hem ended at mid-thigh, gave her friend an indifferent look. 'I don't suppose it matters what you're wearing,' she said carelessly. 'It's okay, I suppose.' She grimaced. 'You'd look good in anything.'

Grace caught her breath. 'That's not true.'

'Yes, it is.' But Julia was complacent. She covered the slight swell of her stomach with a triumphant hand and smiled. 'Thank goodness I saw Matt before you did, hmm?'

Grace hadn't thought she could feel worse, but she did,

73

and she was grateful that Gina spoke to Julia and not to her as they traversed the many halls and corridors of the villa. She tried to find diversion in the many antiquities they passed, several of which were illuminated from above. But although the statues of various Roman gods invited inspection she was intensely aware of the ordeal that lay ahead.

'We're apparently meeting on the *loggia*,' Julia cast back over her shoulder as they descended a flight of stairs to a reception hall that looked suspiciously like the one they'd entered when they'd first come in. She grimaced again. 'Family dinners are obviously less formal. I wanted you to see the drawing room, as well. You wouldn't believe the size of the chandelier they have in there. It's made of Venetian glass.'

'Some other time, perhaps,' Grace managed, somewhat dry-mouthed. 'Um—you won't object, will you, if I slip away after we've eaten?'

Julia shrugged. 'That's up to you,' she said, already quickening her step at the sound of voices. 'My God, so this is what they call the *loggia*! It's not like any verandah I've seen before.'

Grace could have said that that was because it wasn't actually a verandah, but she understood what Julia meant. Huge arched doors gave access to a long vaulted corridor that ran along the back of the villa. Exotic shrubs and trees grew in a variety of stone containers, giving the impression of a tropical garden, while a central fountain played quietly into a marble basin. Wrought-iron lanterns hung from the ceiling and geraniums and scarlet impatiens tumbled from hanging baskets suspended from the walls. The scent of the blossoms was heady, mingling with the smell of citrus that drifted in through windows that were open to the evening air.

Four people awaited them where fan-backed rattan chairs and comfortable loungers flanked a glass-topped iron table, and Grace sensed Julia's jolt of surprise as well as her own as they walked into the room. Fortunately it was almost dark outside so Grace felt sure their reaction would be barely visible to the di Falcos. Nevertheless, it was daunting to discover that it wasn't just the *marchesa* who would be studying their every move.

She saw the *marchesa* at once, of course. Of the two men and two women who were having drinks on the *loggia* she was by far the oldest, seated on a cushioned lounger, with the others gathered about her, like the subjects of some medieval monarch.

Not that Matteo di Falco behaved like any woman's subject, she reflected bitterly. Not unless it suited him to do so. But she couldn't help wondering who the old man was, and why Matteo had told Julia that this was just to be a family dinner.

Predictably, it was Matteo who came to meet them, and Grace was overwhelmingly relieved when he approached Julia first. He wasn't particularly effusive, however, bestowing a polite kiss on each cheek in the continental fashion before turning to Grace. She suffered him to give her a similar salutation, but only she was aware of the possessive pressure of his hands gripping her bare arms and the fact that his mouth lingered rather longer against her cheeks.

Then she was free and he was drawing them towards the others, his manner so cool and controlled that Grace would never have believed that only moments before he had betrayed a quite uncontrollable passion. He scared her, she thought, moving stiffly towards the *marchesa*. Or would it be more accurate to say that her reactions to him scared herself?

'Miss Horton.' While Grace had been lost in the chaos of her own thoughts, Matteo had introduced her to his grandmother, and now the old lady was holding out her hand. 'My grandson has spoken of you,' she added, speaking English, much to Grace's surprise. She smiled. 'I trust our milder climate will prove beneficial to your recuperation.'

Grace was taken aback, and she glanced round for Julia to see if she'd noticed. 'W-well—thank you,' she stammered. 'I am feeling much better already.'

'That's good.' The old lady nodded her approval, and then gestured for the younger woman who was standing beside her to come forward.

'You haven't met my great-granddaughter, have you, Miss Horton?' She smiled up at the girl. 'This is Cecilia.'

'Ceci,' amended the young woman ruefully, and Grace realised that this was who Matteo had been talking about earlier. She reached up and kissed the air at either side of Grace's face. Then she grimaced. 'I wish I was as tall as you.'

'Cecilia!'

The *marchesa* evidently didn't approve of that, but Grace hurried to put her at her ease. 'It's all right,' she said. 'I've always wished that I was small and feminine.'

'I don't think your femininity is in question, *cara*,' Matteo murmured, appearing behind her, and Grace glanced around in alarm, half afraid Julia had overheard him. But her friend apparently knew the other member of the party, and when Matteo introduced his uncle Paolo Grace realised that this must be the 'disgusting' old man Julia had protested about last weekend.

But, in fact, Grace found him a charming old man. He was a little hard of hearing, but she suspected that in his youth he had probably been as attractive to women as his nephew. Certainly, he seemed to find her a delightful companion, and she was only too eager to show Matteo that she preferred his uncle's company to his.

His daughter was another matter, however, and after accepting a glass of wine Grace allowed herself to be drawn back to where Ceci hovered beside her great-grandmother's chair.

'I understand you live in London, Miss Horton,' the old lady commented with interest, but Grace shook her head.

'I *work* in London,' she explained quickly. 'But I live in

Brighton. That's on the south coast, as you probably know. Oh, and please—call me Grace. Miss Horton sounds so formal.'

'Very well.' The *marchesa* inclined her head.

'Wouldn't it be easier if you lived in London, too, as you work there?' asked Ceci artlessly, and suffered another of her great-grandmother's disapproving looks.

'I don't know what the world is coming to, Cecilia!' the old lady exclaimed impatiently. 'In my day, we didn't ask such personal questions.'

'That's all right.' Grace shared a look of understanding with Ceci. 'It's a reasonable question, really...'

'Why do you never say that to me?' asked Matteo softly, coming to stand beside her. He exchanged an enigmatic smile with his grandmother. 'Would anyone like more wine?'

'No, thanks.'

Grace put a protective hand across the rim of her glass just in case he took it into his head to ignore her words, and the *marchesa*'s lips twitched with reluctant amusement. 'What my grandson means is that no one has commented on the quality of the vintage,' she remarked drily. 'This is the '96 pressing, is it not, Matteo? Are you a wine connoisseur, Miss—Grace?'

Grace's lips had parted at her words. 'Do you mean this is your own wine?' she asked involuntarily, and then wished she hadn't sounded so incredulous when she met Matteo's dark gaze.

'Do you like it?' he asked, and Grace had the uneasy feeling that he wasn't just talking about the wine.

'Um—' She looked back at his grandmother for inspiration. 'I—well, yes.'

'It's a new departure for the vineyard,' observed the *marchesa*, holding out her glass to be refilled. 'A Cabernet Sauvignon that incorporates a small amount of our Merlot grapes. Do you know anything about wine-making, Grace?'

'Careful, Nonna,' put in Ceci teasingly. 'That's a leading question.'

'And we never did get an answer to why Grace lives in Brighton when she works in London,' added Matteo, filling his grandmother's glass as he spoke, and proving that he had been aware of their conversation all along. He touched Grace's shoulder with an enquiring finger. 'Isn't that so?'

Grace swallowed. 'My mother lives in Brighton,' she said quickly, addressing herself to the *marchesa*.

'And you live with your mother?' the old lady remarked approvingly. 'How refreshing to meet a young person who doesn't feel it is incumbent upon them to prove their independence by moving out of the family home.'

'It was more a case of Grace moving back into the family home,' Julia commented with some asperity, coming to stand beside Matteo and resting a familiar hand on his shoulder. 'Grace is no angel, are you, darling?'

Grace shook her head. 'No.'

'So what made you decide to move back home?' asked the *marchesa* pleasantly, ignoring the other woman, and Grace wondered if she was the only one who heard Julia's angry intake of breath.

'I—my mother was ill,' she murmured, aware that her friend would think she was milking the situation for all it was worth. 'There was no one else.'

'Only two other sisters,' protested Julia impatiently. 'And I think while you've been here that they've proved that you didn't have to martyr yourself all these years!'

There was an awkward silence after she'd finished and then the *marchesa* reached for her cane that was leaning against her chair. Getting purposefully to her feet, she waved Matteo away when he would have helped her. 'Grace,' she said, gesturing towards her, and Grace could feel the hot colour burning her cheeks at being singled out for attention. 'Will you give me your arm, child? I want to show you something.'

Grace didn't look at Julia as the old lady tucked her hand

under Grace's elbow and directed her to where a cluster of spiny cactus plants hid the flowering succulent that nestled in their midst. 'My husband bought me this plant almost forty years ago, in Bermuda,' she said, with evident pride. 'Beautiful, isn't it? It's called Queen of the Night, and has this distinctive scent that resembles vanilla, don't you think?'

It was a beautiful specimen. Large white flowers that were opening as darkness fell were framed by salmon-coloured petals that radiated around it like a sunflower. Its perfume was unusual and did remind Grace of the scent of vanilla, but she had the uneasy feeling that this was not why the *marchesa* had brought her away from the others.

'Its Latin name is *Selenicereus grandiflorus*,' the old lady went on, 'from which you'll have gathered that it's a member of the Cereus family.' She looked up at Grace. 'Are you interested in horticulture? And can you tell me what your friend expects to achieve by pursuing my grandson?'

Grace blinked. The change of topic had been so sudden that even though she had been half expecting it she was still stunned by the speed of its delivery.

'Julia,' she eventually managed faintly, and the *marchesa* indicated that they should move on.

She paused a few seconds later in front of a Japanese lily. 'So delicate,' she murmured softly, putting out her gnarled fingers and touching its pearl-like blossom. 'I've always been interested in plants. That was why Michele, Matteo's father, had a conservatory built onto the villa. You must let me show it to you some time.' She paused. 'You do know she is pursuing him, don't you?'

Grace swallowed. 'Perhaps he's pursuing her,' she remarked quietly. 'They have been seeing one another for several months.'

'Four months and a handful of days, to be precise,' declared the *marchesa* disparagingly, cutting Julia's estimate by at least eight weeks. 'And for at least half that time Matteo has been trying to extricate himself from her tentacles. But he is too polite to—what is the expression?—tell it how it is?'

Grace nodded. 'Something like that.'

'So, you agree with me?'

'No.' Grace was horrified. 'I just meant, yes, that's what people say.' She inwardly groaned at her own stupidity. 'Um—don't you think your grandson's old enough to—to handle his own affairs?'

The *marchesa* paused to give her another searching look. 'You think this is why I am asking you these questions? Because I am trying to—handle—Matteo's affairs?'

'Well—'

'Oh, no, my dear. You are wrong. Matteo must make his own mistakes.' She drew an audible breath. 'I just thought you might have a vested interest.'

Grace's eyes went wide. 'A vested interest?' she echoed weakly. 'I don't know what you mean.'

'Don't you?' For a moment, Grace thought the old lady was going to accuse her of pursuing Matteo herself. 'Well, Julia is your friend, is she not? You do not strike me as the kind of woman to allow her friend to be hurt unnecessarily, that's all.'

Grace felt as if all the air had been sucked out of her lungs and it was incredibly difficult to articulate a response. 'Perhaps—perhaps you're wrong, Mar—Marchesa,' she stammered, stumbling over the unfamiliar title. It was hard, but it had to be said. 'I—I believe Julia loves your grandson—'

'Love!' The old lady was scornful. 'What is love in today's society? A promise of fidelity—or just an excuse to indulge in pre-marital sex!' Her cane tapped irritably against the ornately tiled floor. 'I may be old, Grace, but I am not unaware of what goes on. And so long as Matteo does not pursue his conquests here—'

'But—'

'No. Listen to me, Grace. I like you, and I think you are an intelligent woman, which is something I cannot say for your friend, regrettably.' She sighed. 'You should know something, however, which you can pass on to your friend or not as you choose. My grandson loved his wife; he loves his daughter. But he does not love your friend. End of story.'

Grace wished it was that simple, but there was something else she wanted to know. 'He—he told me that he does not intend to marry again,' she ventured, and, as she'd hoped, the *marchesa* took her up on it.

'So he says,' she said, with some regret. 'Although, I must confess, I was hoping to change his mind. There was a young woman—' She broke off. 'But that is not what you wish to know, is it, my dear? You are curious as to why Matteo should make such a declaration, and I can tell you it is because of the way Luisa died.' She shook her head with evident sadness. 'Luisa was Cecilia's mother, and she and Matteo were expecting their second child when something went wrong and the baby was born prematurely. Unfortunately, Luisa developed an infection soon afterwards, and although she received the finest care that was available she seemed to fade away before our eyes. Matteo swore then that he would never put another woman through such an ordeal, and if it seems to you that he does not take life very seriously these days, then I must assure you that this is not the case.'

Grace found she had nothing to say. The idea that she could attempt to mediate on Julia's behalf in these circumstances was simply not feasible, and she was inestimably relieved when the *marchesa* suggested that they rejoin the others. 'Signora Carlucci must be almost ready to serve dinner,' she added. 'I must admit, I shall be glad to sit down. These old legs are not what they used to be.'

Julia raised enquiring eyebrows at her friend when they reached the group beside the fountain, but she evidently considered it was more important to retain Matteo's attention than to give in to her obvious curiosity to know what Grace and the *marchesa* had been talking about. It was Ceci

di Falco who left her great-uncle's side and came to take
her great-grandmother's arm. 'Are you all right, Nonna?'
she asked solicitously. 'You're looking a little tired. Is anything wrong?'

'What could be wrong?' demanded the old lady a little
testily. 'I have perhaps been standing for too long. Please
do not make Grace feel as if she is to blame for my short-
comings.' She managed a smile. 'I have been showing her
some of my prized possessions, that is all. I may be wrong,
1but I think she was impressed.'

The arrival of the maid to announce that the meal was
ready curtailed any further conversation, and Grace was
glad when Ceci offered to show her the way. 'Zio Paolo
will escort Nonna,' she said. 'And I'm sure Julia will insist
that Papà takes care of her.' Her lips tightened as they
started out of the *loggia*, and Grace glanced back over her
shoulder in time to see Julia and Matteo exchanging what
appeared to be a few cross words. She shivered and swung
round again just as Ceci added, 'I must say, you're not at
all like Julia, are you? Papà says you're really Dr Horton.
Is that true?'

Although Grace was loath to talk about herself, she was
glad of Ceci's chatter throughout the curiously tense meal
that followed. They ate in what the *marchesa* called the
small dining room, although Grace thought there was nothing particularly small about it. Still, she hesitated to ask
what the other dining room might be like when it was obvious that everything about the villa was built on a grand
scale.

The table they ate at was a huge circle of inlaid mahog-
any with an intricately carved base, from chairs that had
tall carved backs, which had obviously been designed more
for effect than comfort. Even the wall brackets that supported the candle-shaped lamps were carved, too, and
Grace wondered if anyone ever got used to living in a place
like this.

Antipasti was followed by a dish whose main ingredient

appeared to be spinach, and then thin slices of lean beef were served with a red wine sauce. Grace, who wasn't very hungry to begin with, found the food rather too rich for her taste, and she was intensely conscious that Matteo's eyes often rested on her throughout the meal. It was just as well Julia was seated beside him, she thought. In her position, she was unable to see where he directed his gaze when he wasn't looking at her, but Grace had no such advantage, and she almost jumped out of her skin when he spoke to her.

'This is another of our wines,' he said, holding his glass up to the light. The dark red liquid glinted with a subdued brilliance, and Grace felt almost hypnotised by its glowing lustre, concentrating on it rather than on the man who was displaying it. 'It's a Chianti, but we used a white grape to soften its flavour. What do you think?'

'Oh—' Grace felt the hot colour invading her neck and put up her hand to hide her throat. 'I know nothing about wine, *signore*. It—seems very nice.'

'You like it?' the *marchesa* inquired from her position at Grace's right hand, and Grace was forced to concede that she did. 'Good.' The old lady looked pleased. 'But why are you addressing my grandson so formally? I understood from him that you'd seen one another on several occasions before tonight.'

Julia's head jerked round and then, as if suspecting that the *marchesa* was provoking her, she forced a tight smile. 'Just a couple of occasions,' she corrected her, with obvious restraint. 'Isn't that right, Grace? I wouldn't exactly call you and Matt—friends.'

'Oh, but—' began the *marchesa*, clearly about to argue, but Matteo himself intervened.

'I think Grace is just a little shy,' he said smoothly, and Grace realised that he had no intention of exposing his real intentions to his grandmother. He deftly changed the subject. 'By the way, Ceci, I saw Domenico Pasquale in Siena

this afternoon.' His brows arched with warm humour. 'He
wonders why you haven't returned his calls.'

'Oh, Papà—'

'Domenico?' At least the *marchesa* was diverted. 'You
haven't been avoiding Domenico, have you, *cara*?'

Ceci sighed, and Grace felt a surge of sympathy for her.
'No, Nonna—'

'Yet it seems he told your father that you hadn't returned
his calls.' The old lady frowned. 'Is this true?'

Ceci sighed again, and this time her father seemed to
take pity on her. 'I expect Ceci's been so busy with her
end-of-year exams, she hasn't had time to phone all her
friends,' he declared gallantly. His eyes settled on Grace
again, and this time she forced herself not to look away.
'My daughter is a very popular young lady,' he added
mockingly. 'Evidently, she does not take after her father.'

'Oh, Matt!' Julia leaned towards him and put a propri-
etorial hand on his arm. 'You know she's the image of
you.' She circled her lips with the tip of her tongue. 'Stop
teasing Grace. She doesn't like it.'

'I'm sure Grace can answer for herself,' the *marchesa*
put in sharply. 'Ring the bell, Matteo. I think we're all
ready for dessert.'

CHAPTER EIGHT

GRACE was deciding whether to wear trousers or shorts the next morning when she heard someone knocking at her door.

She had taken the precaution of locking the outer door the night before, but although she had lain awake until the early hours no one had disturbed her. Now, however, she quickly stepped into the pale green Bermudas that were easiest to fasten and called nervously, 'Who is it?'

'Who are you expecting?' Julia's response was terse, and Grace searched for an excuse as she opened the door.

'It could have been the maid,' she said, deciding no defence was necessary. And then her expression turned to one of concern. 'What's wrong? You look awful!'

'Oh, boost my confidence, why don't you?' Julia remarked grimly, walking into the parlour with a cold face-cloth pressed to her temple. 'I've got a migraine, what else?' She snorted. 'Isn't that just par for the course? Matt and I get a chance to spend some time together, and I go and ruin everything by getting a headache.'

Grace shook her head. 'Is there anything I can do?'

'Yeah.' Julia slumped down into a velvet-covered armchair. 'Have you got any aspirin or paracetamol that I can take?'

'Oh, but—' Grace caught her lower lip between her teeth. 'Ought you to be taking shop-bought medication?'

'Why not?'

'Well—' Grace hesitated. 'Because of—because of your condition.'

'Oh, I see.' Julia bent forward, resting her head in her

hands. 'Well, I've got to take something. This pain is driving me mad.'

Grace sighed. 'I suppose paracetamol can't do any harm.'

'No, that's right.' Julia lifted her head again in evident relief. 'Do you have some?'

Grace nodded and, going into the bedroom, she found the tape of tablets in her make-up case. Taking them back to her friend, she asked, 'Do you want some water?'

'I suppose so.' Julia was squeezing two of the tablets out of their foil packet. 'God, I'll never drink red wine again.'

Grace came back with a glass of water and stared at her. 'How much did you drink?'

'I don't know.' Julia was offhand now. 'Too much.' She shrugged. 'I suppose that's bad for the baby, too.'

'You know it is.'

'Yes, well, I didn't want Matt wondering why I'd suddenly become a teetotaller, did I?' exclaimed Julia defiantly. 'God, I feel sick!'

'I'm not surprised.'

Grace was finding it difficult to feel any sympathy for her, and her hands balled into fists when Julia suddenly jumped to her feet and sprinted into the bathroom. That she was being sick was evident from the painful retching sounds she was making, and, pushing her own feelings of impatience aside, Grace walked through the bedroom and into the bathroom to offer her help.

Julia was now slumped beside the toilet basin, and Grace couldn't help being moved by her obvious misery. 'You need to go back to bed,' she said gently, wetting one of the hand towels and using it to wipe Julia's damp forehead. 'Come on. You'll feel better soon. My sisters always used to say that mornings were the worst.'

Julia allowed herself to be led back to her own bedroom and helped into bed. She was only wearing a silk robe over her nightdress so it was a simple matter to help her remove it before she sprawled on the sheets.

'You won't tell Matt, will you?' she demanded weakly as Grace covered her with the sheet. 'As far as he's concerned, it's just a migraine, okay? I'll be all right by this afternoon.'

Grace pressed her lips together. 'Can I get you anything else? Some dry toast, perhaps?'

'No. Nothing.' Julia rolled her head from side to side. 'Just keep everyone else out of my way, right? I'm sorry about this, but I can assure you it's not my choice.'

'I know.' Grace decided there was no point in being irritated. 'I'll make your excuses.'

'Thanks.'

Julia nodded, but her eyes were closing, and, realising there was nothing more she could do here, Grace went out and closed the door behind her.

In her own apartments again, she spent a few minutes tidying the bathroom. The last thing she wanted was for the maid to think she had been sick, but she could feel the perspiration already beading between her breasts with the extra exertion. Opening a window, she trusted the sour smell would soon dissipate, and then checked her appearance in the full-length mirror.

Wisps of hair were stuck to her forehead in places, so she used a towel to dry the silvery strands. The friction made them curl against her cheeks instead, and she stared at her reflection with some frustration. With her sparkling eyes and flushed cheeks, she looked little like the serious-minded woman she was used to seeing when she looked in a mirror. But the heat made the idea of wearing trousers totally unfeasible, and she decided that the shorts and black tee shirt would have to do.

Despite her inhibitions, she found her way to the dining room they had used the night before without too much effort. It was easier to get her bearings in daylight, and through the long arched windows that opened onto a sunlit verandah she could see the whole sweep of the valley, and hear the distinctive tolling of a church bell. It was a familiar

sound, yet unfamiliar in these surroundings, and once again
Grace was struck by the natural beauty of the place.

The dining room was deserted, however, and, glancing
at her watch, she saw that it was barely eight o'clock.
Somehow, she'd thought it was much later, and she wondered if she should have waited in her apartments until her
breakfast was brought to her.

Frowning, she wandered out onto the *loggia*, and then
came up short when she saw Matteo di Falco seated at the
table where they'd had drinks the night before, reading a
newspaper. Now the table was spread with a crisp white
cloth, and the jug of orange juice, basket of croissants and
half-empty pot of coffee bore witness to the fact that their
host did not breakfast in bed. The mingled smells of coffee
and warm rolls were mouth-watering, but Grace had the
distinct feeling that she should not be here.

She glanced behind her, estimating her chances of leaving again without him noticing her, and then started when
he said, 'Don't go.' He folded his newspaper, laid it on the
table beside him, and got to his feet. 'Join me.'

'Oh, no—' After what had just happened upstairs, Grace
was in no mood to be civil to the man who was responsible
for it all. 'I—er—I was just looking around, that's all.'

Matteo hooked his thumbs into the back of his belt and
strolled towards her. He was wearing a black tee shirt, too,
this morning, and his arms were brown and muscular beneath the short sleeves. Black jeans hugged his powerful
thighs, and Grace despised herself for the shiver of awareness that feathered her spine at his approach.

'Have you had breakfast?' he asked, arching his dark
brows, and Grace expelled a resigned breath.

'No—'

'I thought not.'

'Well, you would, wouldn't you?' she muttered, pushing
past him and going to stand by the floor-length windows
that overlooked the sunlit gardens. 'You probably know

everything that goes on in the villa,' she added, barely audibly.

'Not everything,' he amended mildly, coming to join her. 'What's the matter? What did I do wrong now?'

Grace snorted. 'Do you have to ask?'

'What?' He was annoyingly tolerant. 'I didn't embarrass you last night, did I?' He blew on her ear. 'I thought I was amazingly restrained in the circumstances.'

Grace jerked her neck away. 'I don't want to be here.'

'No, you told me.' His voice lost a little of its patience. 'That's why I suggest you let me take you somewhere else.'

'Somewhere else?' Grace cast him a disbelieving look. 'Are you crazy?'

'Perhaps.' He stroked a finger along the curve of her chin. 'I'm not suggesting we run away together. I just thought it would be easier for both of us if we were not constantly in the company of other people.'

Grace gaped at him. 'I wouldn't go anywhere with you,' she cried scornfully. 'You have to be out of your mind if you think I'd do that to Julia. Even if I wanted to,' she appended hastily. 'Which I don't.'

Matteo swore then, and although it wasn't a word she'd heard before its meaning was evident. 'Will you stop using Julia's name like some kind of amulet between us?' he demanded. 'Surely you didn't think I encouraged her last night? The way she behaved—that was for your benefit. I have never, at any time, given Julia any reason to think that our association was anything more than a casual—'

'Affair?' suggested Grace disparagingly, and he swore again.

'If you want to call a weekend in Rome an affair, then okay.' He thrust a frustrated hand through his hair, causing it to fall in disarming disarray onto his forehead. 'Grace, you have to believe me here. I am not the—the playboy you are making me out to be.'

He stared at her then, and although she tried to tell herself he was probably the most skilful liar in the world she didn't believe it. Much as she fought against it, she believed him, which made her situation even more impossible than it had been before.

'You do believe me, don't you?' he asked, his voice thickening with emotion, his hand curling round the back of her neck to pull her towards him. And Grace didn't know what might have happened if at that moment she hadn't heard the unmistakable sound of the *marchesa*'s cane tapping across the floor.

'What are you two whispering about?' the old lady demanded huffily, and Grace breathed a prayer of thanks to whatever deity had saved her from making the biggest mistake of her life. Any sympathy she was feeling had to be balanced against the risks he'd taken in having sex with Julia, and if he hadn't wanted the complications he should have made sure that she—that *he*—had some protection.

'I was just trying to persuade Grace to let me show her the monastery of Sant' Emilio,' Matteo responded lightly, his hand falling harmlessly to his side. 'After breakfast, of course. Will you join us, Nonna?' He smiled. 'I know how much you enjoy my company.'

'Will I join you for what?' the old lady asked tersely, though Grace could see she did have a soft spot for her grandson. 'For breakfast? I ate an hour ago. Or an outing to Sant' Emilio? I don't think so. Perhaps you should ask Miss Calloway. She seems to consider that you're the reason she's here.'

There was another of those pregnant pauses, and then Matteo drew an audible breath. 'Perhaps,' he said, turning to Grace. 'Do you know if your friend is awake yet? Shall I ask Gina to find out?'

'No—' Grace's response was urgent, and she was unhappily aware that for a moment he thought she had changed her mind. 'That is—Julia's not very well,' she murmured awkwardly. 'She asked me to offer her apologies. She's going to spend the morning in bed.'

'I see.' The *marchesa*'s gaze moved thoughtfully between them. 'I wonder why. Do you think it was something she ate?'

'Oh, I—'

'Or something she drank, perhaps,' continued the old lady shrewdly. 'I regret to say that Miss Calloway has little regard for her liver.'

'Nonna—'

The *marchesa* knocked away the warning hand Matteo had put on her shoulder. 'I know, I know,' she said crossly. 'Grace is a friend of hers and naturally she does not agree.' She breathed deeply. 'You know, I think I will join you both for coffee, Matteo. Then, before it gets too hot, perhaps Grace would like to walk around the winery with me.'

It was not the most comfortable meal Grace had ever shared, but it was more relaxed than dinner the night before. She found herself telling the *marchesa* more about her work at the museum, how she dealt with the various artifacts that found their way to the museum from digs around the world, and the interesting stories that were attached to exhibits as diverse as ancient Chinese porcelain and the petrified remains of an extinct dinosaur.

The old lady was obviously fascinated by the whole concept of ancient civilisations, and she contributed stories herself about some of the valuable antiques that were housed in the villa. 'I have often thought that they should be catalogued,' she went on thoughtfully. 'Have you ever considered continuing your career in a more individual way, Grace? I am sure there are many owners, like myself, who have libraries and collections that would benefit greatly from your obvious dedication.'

'I think Nonna is offering you a job, *cara*,' remarked Matteo drily, and Grace wondered how she would have felt if she had not been aware of Julia's condition.

'I am merely pointing out what must be obvious to someone of Grace's intelligence,' his grandmother retorted before Grace could speak. 'Come, my dear. Time is pressing.

If you and Matteo intend to visit Sant' Emilio later, we should not waste any more time.'

'Oh, but—'

Grace was about to say that she had no plans for accompanying Matteo to Sant' Emilio when the *marchesa* thwarted her again. 'You do wish to see the winery, don't you?' she asked, apparently misunderstanding her, and Grace sighed.

'Very much,' she conceded through tight lips, but she was aware of Matteo's amusement as she accompanied his grandmother through tall French doors that one of the maids hurried to open at their approach.

It didn't take Grace long to come to the conclusion that the old lady was unlikely to have misinterpreted anything— unless she chose to do so, of course. For a woman who, she surmised, must be in her eighties, she was amazingly astute. All the time she was conducting her guest through the various buildings that made up the winery—where the grapes were crushed and eventually, in the case of the red wines they produced, at least, stored in vats to encourage fermentation—she carried on with the conversation they had earlier been having about Grace's future, gradually learning more and more about her with a skill Grace could only admire.

She was sympathetic when it came to her mother's illness, but she was adamant that Grace had made the right decision in coming away. 'You're too young to be expected to carry the whole burden yourself,' she declared firmly. 'Come; we'll go down to the cellars now. Perhaps Alberto Ponti will permit us to taste the fine brandy he keeps for our special clients.'

It was ten o'clock by the time they returned to the villa, and Grace was concerned that the *marchesa* had done too much. 'Nonsense, child!' the old lady exclaimed, though she did lean rather heavily on the younger woman's arm as they entered the *loggia*. 'If I do not exercise regularly,

I will also become an invalid, and I do not intend to let that happen.'

Grace didn't know whether she felt glad or sorry when she discovered Matteo wasn't waiting for them. The table where they had had breakfast had been cleared, and there was no sign of the disturbing owner of the villa.

'*Caffè—per due,*' the *marchesa* ordered of the maid who appeared to ask if there was anything her mistress needed, and although Grace had no desire for any more caffeine she could hardly leave the old lady on her own.

The *marchesa* made herself comfortable on the cushioned lounger she had occupied the night before, but Grace was too much on edge to sit down. Where was Matteo? she wondered. Had he gone to check on Julia himself? And if so, ought she to be loitering here, as if she was obediently waiting for his return?

'You say Miss Calloway intends to spend the day in bed?' the *marchesa* enquired pleasantly, and Grace wondered if she was only imagining the note of satisfaction in the old lady's voice.

'Just the morning, I think,' she answered, touching the leaves of a bell-shaped fuchsia that hung from one of the baskets that was espaliered to the wall. She found she couldn't look the *marchesa* in the eye, and, wrapping her arms about her midriff, she added, 'Perhaps I should go and see how she is.'

'I'm sure Miss Calloway will join us as soon as she's able,' declared the old lady repressively, thereby putting an end to that suggestion. 'Ah, here's Matteo.' She gave her grandson a speaking look. 'We were beginning to wonder if you'd changed your mind.'

Grace had wondered no such thing; quite the contrary, in fact. She'd been hoping he had thought better of his invitation, but judging by the look he cast in her direction she'd been wasting her time.

'A small problem with the irrigation system, Nonna,' he averred, his presence immediately dispelling any relief

Grace might have been feeling. 'Happily, Aldo was able to repair it, and I am now at Grace's disposal.'

'Oh, really——' Grace began, only to have the *marchesa* override her automatic objection.

'Nonsense, child,' she said. 'The outing will do you good.' She smiled, folding her hands together in her lap. 'I'll tell Miss Calloway where you've gone if she puts in an appearance before you get back.'

Grace pressed her lips together. 'Well...' She hesitated. 'Maybe after we've had coffee...'

'I'm sure you were only joining me for coffee because you were too polite to refuse,' declared the old lady shrewdly. 'Go along now. I'll see you both at lunch, I hope.'

Matteo's car was waiting outside, and this time he didn't make the mistake of allowing her to avoid his courtesy. Striding ahead of her, he had the door open before she reached the car, exchanging a mocking glance with her as she got rather ungraciously into the passenger seat.

'Smile,' he advised as he got in beside her. 'Nonna may be watching. You don't want her to think you're only humouring her by coming with me, do you?'

Grace sniffed. 'Even if I am.'

'Even if you are,' he conceded, putting the car into gear. 'Come on, *cara*. I'm sure you don't hate me half as much as you pretend.'

'Don't bet on it,' muttered Grace, turning her head away, but she heard the soft chuckle he gave as he accelerated down the long avenue of trees.

The ruined monastery of Sant' Emilio wasn't far from the villa as the crow flies, but the journey took considerably longer by road. It was situated high in the hills that overlooked the valley, and the route they took was little more than a goat track in places. Grace couldn't help but admire the view as they climbed the mountainous passes, but she found herself gripping her seat with sweating hands as the

car skimmed the narrow ridge that wound up to the building's crumbling walls.

'We'll make it,' remarked Matteo gently, noticing her
terror, and she forced herself to relax as they reached the
stone gateway that had once given access to the inner courtyard of the monastery. 'Imagine what it must have been
like for the monks, having to bring all their supplies up in
a cart or on the back of a mule. Whatever protection its
remoteness gave them must have been far exceeded by its
inaccessibility.'

Grace nodded, but when Matteo stopped the car she
made no immediate attempt to move. She wasn't at all sure
her legs would support her, and she let Matteo get out and
disappear through the weather-scarred archway before
opening her door.

She was leaning against the engine-warmed bonnet of
the vehicle when he came back to see why she hadn't followed him. It was considerably cooler here and the heat of
the car was pleasant against her bare thighs. But she was
instantly aware of his appraisal, and she gave him a defensive look.

'It's a marvellous view,' she said, trying not to think
about the fact that they had to descend by the same route
as they'd come up, and Matteo pushed his hands into the
pockets of his jeans as he strolled towards her.

'Some compensation, I suppose,' he agreed, gazing about
him. 'But the monks who ran this place weren't interested
in secular pleasures. They were Cistercians, who are believed to have come here in the twelfth century. They were
the followers of a saint who taught self-sufficiency and aus-
terity above all things.'

Grace nodded. 'What else?'

Matteo's lips twitched. 'Are you feeling better?'

Grace pushed herself up from the car. 'I feel fine.'

'Oh, good.' He was sardonic. 'I thought for a minute that
you were nervous.' He came towards her, but although she
stiffened automatically he only pointed down into the val-

ley below them. 'There's the villa,' he said, and she swallowed convulsively. It looked like a doll's house, set in a
field of green.

'Stop worrying,' he said, and she realised she wasn't
fooling him for a minute. 'Come on. I'll show you the altar
in the chapel that's still standing. Well, part of it is, anyway,' he amended as he guided her through the arched
gateway. 'As you can imagine, we don't get many tourists
making the trek up to the monastery. I guess that's why it's
still here. So many old buildings have crumbled beneath
the weight of their own popularity.'

Grace marvelled that anyone could have conceived of
building in such a place. The monastery's outer walls were
simply an extension of the rocky hillside in places, with
drops of hundreds of feet falling away below.

It was certainly not the sort of place for someone who
suffered from vertigo, but, even though she'd never considered herself a victim before, gazing down such precipitous slopes did make her feel a little dizzy. Maybe it was
the prospect of their return journey still lingering in the
back of her mind, she thought tensely. Whatever the reason,
she tried to stay well away from the curtain walls.

'Come and see this,' Matteo called as she was resting on
a pile of stones in the middle of what he had told her used
to be the refectory. He beckoned her to where he was standing at the far end of the ruined dormitory. 'Don't be scared.
I won't let you fall.'

'I'm not scared,' Grace declared irritably, but she approached him with obvious reluctance, looking anywhere
but at the ledge where he was sitting.

'If you say so,' he remarked wryly, reaching out and
grasping her hand. 'Come here. I'm not going to push you
over.'

Grace went, but slowly, hardly aware of the hands that
curved round her bare thighs as he drew her between his
knees. 'There,' he said softly, pointing towards a pine-
covered ridge that speared up out of the hillside above

them. 'Can you see the nest? It's a hawk's. Look, there seem to be several young birds inside.'

Grace gasped. 'Oh, yes. Yes, I can see it.' She put her fingers to her lips in wonder. 'Heavens, how ever did you know it was there?'

'I didn't. But I was watching a hawk flying around the ridge, and then it swooped down with something in its beak.' He shook his head. 'I knew there were hawks nesting in the valley,' he added modestly. 'But I've never seen a nest before.' He turned her round to face him. 'That's what *falco* means, of course.'

'Of course.'

Grace looked down at him in sudden comprehension, and at the same moment she became aware of his strong fingers gripping her legs beneath the hem of her shorts. She stepped back instinctively, not giving a thought to what was behind her, and then flapped her arms in panic, when the ground crumbled beneath her feet.

Matteo's actions were swift and automatic. Although she realised later that she had never been in any real danger, because the ledge would have saved her, when he reached for her she clutched his arms with desperate fingers. He pulled her sideways, away from the opening, and she was overwhelmingly relieved when she felt the wall of a chimney at her back.

'Oh, God!' She was shuddering uncontrollably, and Matteo's hands cupped her neck in gentle reassurance.

'You're okay,' he said, smoothing back the strands of damp hair that were clinging to her forehead. 'I promised you I wouldn't let you fall.'

'That—that's easy for you to say,' she muttered, trying to sound flippant and failing abysmally. 'I thought—I thought—'

'I know what you thought,' he assured her huskily, pressing one finger against her quivering lips. 'But it didn't happen. Nor would it, believe me!' His eyes darkened with sudden emotion. 'I'd never let anything bad happen to you.'

Grace's breath caught in her throat, and, realising she was still grasping his arms in a death-like grip, she forced her fingers to part. 'Well—thank you,' she said, intensely conscious of his nearness. 'But I don't think you can be sure of that.'

'Why not?'

'Why not?' She tried to look over his shoulder, but her eyes were drawn to the compelling beauty of his. 'Well, because it's just one of those things people say. When I leave here, you won't have any control over my life.'

'Ah...' His eyes dropped to her mouth, and she pressed her shoulders back against the wall in an effort to hold onto reality. 'When you leave here. I see.' His thumbs caressed her cheeks. 'And what if I don't want to let you go?'

Grace shivered. She had to think of Julia, she told herself. She had to remember why he had brought her here, and the contempt she'd felt for the way he was treating her friend.

But...

'I think your grandmother would have something to say about that, don't you?' she got out, despising herself for her weakness. 'And—and your daughter?'

Not to mention the child he as yet knew nothing about! But she couldn't say that.

'Why do you always make excuses for the way you feel?' he demanded, his hands trailing sensuously down the slender column of her throat to her heaving chest. He spread his fingers, deliberately brushing the swollen peaks of her breasts that pushed treacherously against the soft cotton of her tee shirt. 'You know you want me to touch you. And God knows,' he groaned as he glanced down between his legs, 'I want you to touch me.'

'No—'

'Yes,' he insisted, moving closer, and she felt the hardness of his arousal against her stomach. 'Open your mouth.'

She knew she should stop him. She knew she was only building up a whole heap of trouble for herself by even allowing him to get this close to her, but she watched his dark head descend towards hers with a feeling of helpless inevitability. She wanted him to kiss her, she couldn't deny it, and if that meant she would be damning herself to a lonely, loveless future, then so be it. Julia would never know about it. Not from her. And what was a kiss anyway to a man like him?

She soon found out.

When his mouth parted over hers, when his tongue thrust sinuously between her teeth, her knees turned to water beneath her. He'd kissed her before; of course he had. That evening in his car was not so far distant that she couldn't remember every moment of that almost experimental embrace. But this was different. This was raw, and this was dangerous, and she didn't realise her mistake until it was too late to do anything about it.

A flame, hot and uninvited, ignited inside her, so that she had to clutch a handful of his shirt to save herself from falling. His hand at her nape tilted her head back against the wall, but she was hardly conscious of its uneven surface against her scalp. All she was really aware of was the hungry possession of his mouth, and the devouring need she had to arch against him until the muscled contours of his body crushed hers to the wall behind her.

'*Dio*, Grace,' he muttered, lapsing into a spate of passionate Italian she couldn't begin to understand, before seeking her mouth again.

The excitement built up inside her as he punished her lips with a hungry intensity she'd never known before. His tongue meshed with hers, drawing it into his mouth so that he could suck mindlessly on the tip. He bit her lips, nibbling the vulnerable inner flesh with his teeth, but she was hardly aware of it. Her head was swimming, with a dozen different emotions vying for supremacy, and she could only reach up and hold onto his neck as the one stable thing in a rapidly changing world.

The first intimation she had that he had tugged the hem

of her tee shirt out of the waistband of her shorts was when she felt his hands against her bare flesh. Her spine recoiled from the unexpected familiarity, but when his thumbs brushed the soft undersides of her breasts she didn't pull away.

Strong fingers stroked her midriff before sliding under the elasticised strap of her bra. The catch gave way so easily she guessed he must have had plenty of experience in this kind of situation. But even though she knew she ought to break free his thumbs had found her engorged nipples and she doubted her legs would hold her.

It had to end. Even as she heard the plaintive cry of the hawk overhead, protesting that they were invading its territory, another sound came to her ears. It was the distinctive rattle of the bells the goats wore around their necks, and she had hardly made the identification before Matteo was pulling away.

'Damnation,' he said, and this time she did understand him. But thankfully the strength had also returned to her legs, and by the time the goatherd appeared to round up his flock she had fastened her bra again with trembling fingers and was examining her braid for damage.

She turned away as Matteo spoke to the man. She had no wish for him to see her face and possibly speculate on why she was so flushed or how her mouth had got to be bare of make-up. And swollen? she fretted, running anxious fingers over her tender lips. Dear God, she probably looked as if Matteo had been having sex with her, and in a sense he had. It was only the chance appearance of the goatherd and his flock that had saved her from total humiliation.

CHAPTER NINE

SHE didn't speak to Matteo again until they were back in the car and even then she did so with a feeling of bitter self-disgust.

'I suppose that's why you brought me here,' she said tightly. 'What a pity that old man had to come along and thwart your plans.'

For once, Matteo didn't have a ready answer for her. 'I didn't have any plans,' he said flatly, glancing her way. 'Fasten your seatbelt. The road's equally rocky going down as it was coming up.'

'I know that.'

But at least what had happened had robbed her of any fear for her own safety. Indeed, there were times during that arduous journey when she half wished that Matteo was not such a good driver. A careless swing of the wheel, and they'd have been sailing out into space with the certain assurance of death at the foot of each precipitous drop. If it wasn't for her mother, she would have nothing to lose. She'd already lost her self-respect.

But as they neared the gates of the villa other anxieties reasserted themselves. 'What do I look like?' she asked, looking at Matteo, and his face lost its grim expression.

'How you always look,' he told her, a certain roughness to his voice. 'Beautiful—'

'That's not what I meant!' exclaimed Grace frustratedly. 'I'm not looking for compliments here. Particularly not from you!' She took a breath. 'I want you to tell me honestly how I look. Will—will anyone—will anyone be able to tell—?'

'That I've been kissing you?' Matteo broke in wryly. 'Is

that all that worries you? Whether anyone's likely to find out?'

'Frankly, yes.' Grace gave a sudden shiver of remembrance. 'I knew it. I knew I should never have gone with you. Whatever your grandmother might have thought, I should have stuck to my own beliefs.'

'Why?' The avenue of poplars could be seen ahead of them now. 'Didn't you enjoy any of it?'

'No—'

'Not even the hawk?'

'Oh—' Grace made a fluttery little gesture. 'Well, yes. Seeing the hawk was a thrill, but—but how was I to know you were going to use it to—to—?'

'Have my wicked way with you?' he suggested, with bitter humour. 'Get real, Grace. I didn't know you were going to do an imitation of a bungee-jumper, without the rope.'

Grace gave him a resentful look. 'I should have known you'd make fun of me.'

'I'm not making fun of you,' he protested wearily. 'But as far as I'm concerned there are more significant implications here than whether I took advantage of the situation.'

'Oh, yes,' Grace agreed. 'Like what you intend to do about Julia, for example.'

'Julia?' He looked genuinely puzzled. 'No, Grace. Not Julia. You. What I'm going to do about you. It's not something I'd ever thought I'd have to deal with, but it seems I must.'

'Don't bother.' Grace was panic-stricken at the thought that he might be going to tell Julia that he'd decided to transfer his unwelcome attentions to *her*. But they were driving down the avenue of trees now, and the villa was approaching fast, so this was not the time to start that kind of conversation. Her nails curled painfully into her palms. 'You never did tell me how I look.'

'Fine,' he said harshly, clearly irritated by her determination not to share his concerns. 'You look fine. What would you rather have me say? That anyone looking at you would know what we'd been doing?'

Grace breathed convulsively. 'Would they?'

Matteo scowled. 'We'll soon find out,' he declared brusquely. 'There seems to be a welcoming committee waiting on the terrace.'

She thought he was just trying to frighten her, but in fact the other members of the house party were gathered on the terrace having pre-lunch drinks as they drove up. The *marchesa* was there, and Ceci, and Uncle Paolo, and just when Grace was beginning to breathe a little more easily she saw Julia, too. Her friend was lounging on a chair that was set in the shade of an enormous flower-patterned parasol, and that was why she hadn't been immediately visible.

Grace wanted to die. She had hoped she might be able to get to her room without seeing anyone, but she realised now that that had just been an impossible dream. Apart from anything else, nothing went on at the Villa di Falco without the *marchesa* knowing about it, and judging by the look of satisfaction on her face she had lost no time in telling Julia where they'd gone.

Matteo was obliged to park the car on the sweep of forecourt that lay to one side of the terrace, and he cast a look of helpless resignation in Grace's direction as he made to get out of the car.

'Not my fault,' he said flatly, and then turned as Ceci came running to meet them.

'Where have you been?' she demanded, tucking her hand through her father's arm. 'You've been ages. Zio Paolo was sure you must have had an accident.'

Matteo's smile was forced. 'But you knew where we'd gone? Nonna told you.'

'Oh, yes.' Ceci had a smile for Grace as she came, reluctantly, to join them. 'She said you'd gone to Sant' Emilio. I wish I'd known you were going. I'd have gone with you.'

'No, you wouldn't.' Matteo met Grace's shocked gaze

with a mocking stare. 'Have you forgotten, *cara*? The car is only a two-seater.'

'Oh...' As Ceci absorbed what her father had said, Grace realised that once again Matteo had been baiting *her*. 'Well, we could have taken one of the other automobiles, then,' the girl persisted. 'The Rolls, *forse*? Or the Mercedes?'

'Ah, yes.' Matteo's tone was dry. 'And do you think Nonna would condone me taking one of her vehicles up to the monastery?'

'Maybe not.'

Ceci evidently decided to abandon the argument, and in any case they were already starting up the two shallow steps to the terrace. As they did so, Julia, also, got out of her chair, and Grace prepared herself for a different kind of protest.

But before Julia could say anything the *marchesa* took centre stage. 'You look flushed, child!' she exclaimed, giving her grandson a reproving look. 'Matteo, I hope you haven't kept Grace too long in the sun.'

'Really, I'm fine—' began Grace, only to break off in confusion when Matteo bent to give his grandmother a salutatory kiss. His hand had brushed the swell of her taut buttocks in passing, and although no one else had seen it she couldn't believe it had been accidental.

'I'm sure Grace will tell you that I took very good care of her, Nonna,' he murmured smoothly. 'But in an open car...'

'It is a problem, I agree.' The *marchesa* nodded as Matteo stepped aside. 'But perhaps she would like to freshen up before we eat? I'm sure we can all wait a few minutes longer for our lunch.'

She was looking at her now, and Grace wondered if the old lady had any idea how grateful she was for the favour. 'I would,' she said at once, starting towards the door. 'Thank you.'

Viewing her reflection a few minutes later, Grace was relieved to see she didn't look half as bad as she'd expected. She did look a little flushed, as the *marchesa* had said, but she wore very little make-up anyway, so its absence was hardly a tragedy. What disturbed her more was the unfamiliar wildness of her eyes. If anyone cared to look, they were a mirror of the agitation she was feeling inside, and she spent some minutes bathing them with cold water before tackling her hair.

She saw, with mixed feelings, that Matteo was talking to Julia when she rejoined the others. She hoped he was redeeming his neglect of her that morning, but she was afraid he might be doing just the opposite. After the way she'd behaved, she could hardly look her friend in the eye, and blaming Matteo for everything just didn't cut it. Julia had every right to despise both of them and as soon as this weekend was over she was going back to England.

She knew Julia would have something to say about her going off with her boyfriend and she got her chance after lunch. The *marchesa* usually rested in the afternoon and Matteo's uncle decided to do the same. Matteo had estate matters to attend to, or so he said, and Ceci disappeared also, which left the two women alone on the *loggia*.

It could have been very pleasant, Grace reflected ruefully. They'd returned to the *loggia* after lunch because it was cooler. Its high arched ceiling and thick walls gave protection from the somnolent heat that hung over the valley, and in other circumstances she would have been quite content to while the afternoon away reading or simply relaxing on the cane chairs. But Julia wanted to talk, she knew it, and she couldn't altogether blame her.

'Did you tell him?'

Julia's first words when they were alone startled Grace into an unwary exclamation. 'Tell him?' she echoed. 'Tell him what?'

'Think,' said Julia flatly. 'Why I was ill, of course.'

'No.' Grace was glad she could be completely honest. 'I just said you had a headache, that's all.'

'Hmm.' Julia didn't sound convinced. 'So why was he so solicitous of my welfare when you got back?'

'Well...' How to answer that? 'I don't know. He was concerned about you, I suppose. Why do you think?'

'I don't know.' Julia was doubtful. 'I don't always understand him.' She grimaced. 'Well, he is three-quarters Italian, I suppose.'

Grace nodded, hoping to change the subject. 'What time did you get up?'

'Oh, no.' Julia held up her hands. 'We're not going to leave it there. I want to know what you thought you were playing at, going off with him like that. It wasn't your place to monopolise his whole morning. I felt like an interloper when I came downstairs and found only Matteo's grandmother and his uncle sitting on the terrace.'

Grace sighed. 'I'm sorry.'

'So you should be. I didn't bring you here to make my life more difficult than it already is. You still haven't told me how you came to go out with Matt in the first place. Did you ask him to take you sightseeing?'

'No!' Grace was indignant. 'Of course I didn't *ask* him. But he mentioned the monastery, and the *marchesa*—'

'Oh, yeah!' Julia snorted. 'I might have known that old woman had a hand in it.' She shook her head. 'Poor Matt! I bet she put him on the spot, didn't she? She's always doing that.'

Grace couldn't honestly say she'd noticed, but if Julia wanted to believe that the *marchesa* had organised the whole thing, then so be it. She had other, less easy matters to discuss with her.

'Look at when you got back earlier,' Julia went on disparagingly. 'It wasn't Matt's fault that you were stupid enough to go out without a hat, but did his grandmother see it that way? Oh, no.' She made a derisive sound. 'The sooner she's shunted off to a retirement home, the better!'

'Oh, but—'

Grace had been about to say that she was sure Matteo

would never agree to exiling his grandmother from the place that had been her home for over sixty years, but she thought better of it. What did she really know about Matteo, when all was said and done? Just what he'd chosen to tell her. And if half of what Julia had said about their relationship was true, she didn't know him at all.

'I mean it.' Julia was speaking again. 'This villa simply isn't big enough for the two of us, and if Matt and I are to get married—'

'But are you? Are you sure that's what you want to do?' Grace turned impulsively towards her friend, and although she could see that what she was saying was not being well received she had to go on. 'I mean it, Julia. These people— well, they're very nice, of course, but do you really think you would be happy living here? I mean, it's not what you're used to, is it? I always thought you preferred the town to the country, and there are no nightclubs here—'

'There are in Portofalco. Places with music, anyway. And besides, Matt has an apartment in Florence. That was where he was staying when I met him.'

Grace shook her head. 'I don't think you've thought this through.'

'What do you mean?'

'You're going to have a baby, Julia. Someone's going to have to look after it. Not to mention the fact that you're going to have to feed it—'

'If you think I'd feed a baby myself, you've got another think coming!' exclaimed Julia incredulously. 'My baby will have a nanny and it will be bottle-fed, right from the start.'

'And what if Matteo doesn't agree with your arrangements? What then?'

'What is this?' Julia was staring at her now. 'What has he been saying?'

'Matteo?' Grace made a helpless gesture. 'What could he say? He doesn't even know about the baby, does he?'

'No. So why are you so knowledgeable all of a sudden?

Does sucking up to the *marchesa* give you some divine right to interfere in my affairs?'

'No.' Grace was horrified. 'And I haven't been sucking up to the *marchesa*.'

'Haven't you?' Julia was bitter. 'So how come she always speaks in English when you're around?'

'I don't know.' Grace couldn't pretend she hadn't noticed. 'Perhaps it's because she knows I don't understand Italian. Whereas you do.'

'How would she know that? I don't remember you telling her.'

'Well…' Grace was stumped. She could hardly suggest that Matteo might have told her without inviting more questions. She compromised. 'You must have told Matteo yourself.'

Julia frowned, but clearly that suggestion had more merit. 'Perhaps,' she conceded slowly. 'Anyway, we're getting away from the real substance here. Why these doubts about whether or not Matt and I should get married? What's it to you?'

Grace sighed. 'I just want to be sure you know what you're doing, that's all. Have you discussed this with your mother?'

'*With my mother!*' Julia was scornful. 'Since when have Madeline and I discussed anything? D'you think I want to be like her?' She scoffed. 'Forget it.'

Grace shrugged. Perhaps that hadn't been the wisest suggestion, she acknowledged. Julia's parents had split up when she was a baby, and she had never really known her father. Madeline Calloway had farmed her daughter out to anyone who would look after her, and by the time Julia was a teenager they had become virtual strangers to one another.

'Anyway, of course I know what I'm doing,' Julia declared now. 'I'm going to marry Matt. I'd be a fool not to.'

'Because you're pregnant?'

'Well, that would seem to me to be a pretty good reason,

don't you think?' Julia asked sarcastically. 'Or are you suggesting I'd be better off as a one-parent family?' She gave Grace a belittling look. 'Sorry, girl, but I'm not particularly interested in being a *mother*!' She grimaced. 'I just want to know that whatever happens in the future I shan't ever have to worry about—well, about security again.'

Grace blew out a breath. 'You mean money, don't you?'

'All right.' Julia didn't argue. 'I mean money.' She shrugged unrepentantly. 'Do you have any conception of how much the di Falcos are worth?'

Grace lifted her shoulders. 'A lot, I suppose.'

'You're not wrong.' Julia spread her arms wide. 'Just think about it. This villa must be worth millions of lire.'

Grace pulled a wry face. 'That's not saying a lot.'

'All right, know-it-all. Millions of pounds, then. You're an expert. You must know that the artwork alone is worth a fortune.'

'So what?'

'So what?' Julia's jaw dropped. 'Come on, Grace, level with me. Would you turn down an offer like that?'

Grace breathed a little unevenly. 'He's asked you to marry him already?'

'No.' Julia looked impatient. 'Matt's far too crafty for that. Oh, yes,' she said as Grace looked shocked, 'I know it's not going to be easy, despite what I said before. He warned me at the beginning that he had no intention of getting married again.'

'Oh, Julia!'

'Don't look at me like that, Grace. All men are wary of committing themselves to marriage. Heavens, with our experiences, you should know that. As a matter of fact, Ray— you remember my first husband?—he didn't want to get married either. I'm afraid we have that kind of effect on men, girl. I guess you've decided you're never going to make the grade.'

Julia was blunt, but Grace couldn't entirely blame her for that. Besides, it was true. Men did only want one thing from her, Matteo included. Which made the idea of his marriage to Julia even more distasteful. How could anyone trust a man like that?

'I just think you might be making a big mistake,' she said flatly. 'Do think about it, Julia. You know I'll help you, if I can.'

'How?' Julia was sardonic. 'By adding me to your list of good causes?' She gave a short laugh. 'No, thanks, Grace. I think you've got all the lame ducks you can handle.'

Grace pressed her lips together. 'My mother is not a lame duck,' she protested, stung into a heated defence.

'Well, you always put more store in family relationships than I did,' replied Julia dismissively. 'Which reminds me, what did you think of the *enfant terrible*? I could do without her always hanging about Matt. Of course, she and the old lady are thick as thieves.'

'I liked her,' said Grace at once. 'And she's a student, Julia. It's natural that she wants to spend some time with her father while she's at home.'

'Well, I notice you managed to shake her off this morning,' retorted Julia caustically. 'Oh, God, here she comes. I think I'll go and have a bath.'

CHAPTER TEN

GRACE was dreaming.

She dreamed she was at the monastery again, only now it was dark. A thin sickle moon, riding in and out of the racing clouds, provided the only real illumination, but the huge cavern of sky over her head was filled with stars. The air was soft and warm, much warmer than she remembered, the ruined walls of the old building silhouetted against the sky, stark, yet eerily beautiful. She wasn't afraid; on the contrary, she felt strangely powerful. No longer bound by earthly ties but at one with the night.

She dreamed she was standing in what had once been the refectory, where the stones beneath her feet were overgrown with coarse grass. Her feet were bare, she noticed, but she didn't feel any discomfort. Her toes curled into the cool turf, loving the feeling of freedom it gave her.

It was only as the breeze stirred the hem of the overlarge tee shirt she had been wearing to sleep in that she realised that it wasn't just her feet that were bare. Beneath the shirt, cool air curled intimately between her bare thighs, and she lifted her arms above her head and spun around in an uncontrolled display of excitement.

She didn't know when she became aware that she wasn't alone. It could have been when the action of raising her arms above her head caused the hem of the tee shirt to ride up her bare thighs, or perhaps she heard the whisper of a breath as someone else breathed the warm air. Whatever, like a cloud across the moon, she was aware of an alien presence, and she turned slowly towards the break in the wall where she and Matteo had watched the hawk that morning.

And he was there, as she had somehow known he would be, lounging on the ledge, one leg drawn up to provide a resting-place for the arm that supported his chin. Unlike her, he was fully dressed: all in black, as he'd been that morning, sleek and dark and sexy, and unnervingly familiar.

Her heartbeat quickened; she could feel it. Could feel every pulse in her body responding to his effortless appeal, so that when he held his hand out towards her she had to dig her heels into the soft earth to stop herself from drifting towards him.

But she wanted to go to him. Lord, did she ever! The pulse between her legs was the most insistent of all, and she could feel the moisture pooling between her thighs. She knew what that meant, knew what she needed, but there were barriers between them, and although she couldn't remember what they were at this precise moment they were strong enough to keep her where she was.

'Don't be afraid,' he said, and when she still didn't go to him he got up from the ledge and came towards her. 'You know you came here looking for me.'

'I didn't!'

Grace was horrified that he should think such a thing, but he only laughed softly at her indignant response. 'Of course you did,' he said, halting in front of her. 'And I came here looking for you, so that makes us equal.'

Grace swallowed. 'What do you want?'

'What do *you* want?'

'Me?' She gazed at him in confusion. 'I don't know what you mean.'

'I think you do.' The tips of his fingers trailed the length of her arm. 'That's why you're here. It's no use denying it. Your body gives you away every time.'

'You don't know anything about my body.'

'Don't I?' His fingers had reached the hem of her tee shirt. 'I know you're trembling, and that your heart's beating at twice its normal rate. That's enough to be going on with.'

'Oh, please—' When his hand touched her bare thigh, she jumped back in alarm. 'Please, you mustn't.'

'Mustn't I?' His eyes held hers with a mesmerising intensity. 'Why not? There's no one else here.'

'Because it's wrong—'

'Why? Why is it wrong?' He bent his mouth to her neck and she felt his teeth bruising her soft skin. 'It seems eminently right to me.' His tongue caressed the abrasion his teeth had made. 'There: now I've put my mark on you.'

'Oh, no—' Grace's hand went at once to discover what he had done, and she was hardly aware of him lifting the hem of her shirt until she felt his hand against her bare flesh. 'Matteo, please...'

'What?' He brushed her mouth with sensual lips. 'Don't you want me to touch you? Don't you want me to look at you? You're beautiful, *cara*. Don't be afraid of your body.'

'I'm—I'm not—afraid,' she got out jerkily, but she was and she knew it. Her body had betrayed her before; she couldn't exactly remember when, but it had. And she also knew she must not let it betray her again.

'Then let me do what I want to do to it,' he said huskily, and although she wanted to resist she felt him part her trembling legs.

But when he cupped her mound in his hand she knew he must be able to feel her arousal. And when his fingers came away wet with her essence she was mortified.

Yet when Matteo sought her mouth again her lips parted in helpless abandon, and when he eased the tee shirt higher so that he could weigh her full breasts in his hands she could only share his satisfaction. Her swollen nipples thrust against his palms, and he murmured his approval, groaning a little when she arched against him and felt the rigid shaft of his arousal straining his zip.

And, although she knew she was playing with fire, Grace's hands found the buckle of his belt and loosened it.

Then, with the utmost temerity, she eased the zip down over his tumescent flesh and discovered that he wasn't wearing any underwear either. Which was as it should be, she thought. The slick throbbing length of him spilled into her hands, and he gave an anguished moan when she stroked his silky skin.

'Easy, *cara*,' he whispered thickly, and then somehow they were lying on the stones, and she was murmuring little sounds of pleasure at this evidence of his vulnerability.

The stones were warm, too, or perhaps it was just the heat of their bodies, Grace mused, accepting the fact that Matteo was naked now. She felt a moment's discomfort as he tore her hair out of its braid and spread it out around her, but she revelled in its freedom and it was soon forgotten.

He was hot, so hot, his hair-roughened thigh sliding between hers to knead that most sensitive part of her anatomy. There was hair on his chest, too, arrowing down below his navel, and it tickled her tender breasts, his nipples button-hard beneath her questing fingers. She'd never known a man whose body pleased her so much, and she wriggled provocatively beneath him, inciting him even more.

He murmured to her in his own language, smoothing the silvery curls from her forehead with his lips, trailing strands across her mouth and kissing her with its silken coils between them. He kissed the soft mounds of her breasts, lifting her nipples to his mouth, and suckling from each of them in turn.

Grace felt a sharp pain in the pit of her stomach, and when he moved lower, tracing the quivering muscles of her midriff with his lips, she moaned in sweet abandon. Her protests died in her throat as his mouth found the moist curls that guarded the apex of her thighs, and his tongue brought her to a shuddering climax without any apparent effort on his part.

Yet, still, her body ached for a more complete satisfaction. As the spreading ripples of emotion stirred again, she couldn't wait for him to take his own release. She had thought there could be no more profound pleasure than that which he had already given her, but when he parted her legs and the throbbing pulse of his manhood nudged the drenched folds of her sex she closed her eyes in mindless anticipation.

She wanted him to enter her. She wanted the pulsating thickness of him to part and stretch her, to fill that aching place inside her that she'd never known she had before. She wanted the powerful thrust of his body in her and over her, for him to make himself a part of her and her a part of him.

But nothing happened.

Even though she tossed and turned in anguished need, he held back from her, and she wanted to die. She tried to open her eyes and see for herself what it was that was stopping him, but they felt as if they were glued shut, and, no matter how she tried, she couldn't lift her lids. She tried to speak, to beg him to take pity on her, to tell him that she didn't care about anything any more, that they were soulmates, that they were meant to be together, but she was dumb. And when she reached out to him her hands met only emptiness. He wasn't there.

Panic set in. Her struggles became more frantic, and she found she was wrapped up in some confining cloth that was acting like a binding sheet around her sweating limbs.

A cry rose up in her throat and with an almighty thrust she tore free of the restriction and dragged herself up—

In bed!

Trembling, as much from the horror of what her subconscious had created as from her exertions, Grace stared tremulously about her. The bed was a shambles. The sheet, which must have been what had imprisoned her, was torn away from the mattress, and she was still hugging the pillow she had evidently believed was Matteo in her dream.

A groan of revulsion escaped her, and she flung the pillow aside in disgust. Dear God, what was happening to her?

She had never experienced anything like it before, and she dropped her head into her hands as a feeling of utter devastation engulfed her.

And realised that her hair was loose! It hung in tangled confusion about her shoulders, and just for a moment she wondered if it had been a dream after all. Could he—could he possibly have come here...?

But no. Her lips twisted. She was merely clutching at straws, trying to find some way to excuse her own behaviour. Apart from anything else, she'd locked the door again before she'd gone to bed, and there was no way Matteo could have got into the room without her knowing about it. Besides, if he had, why would he have stopped when he did? Given her pathetic lack of resistance, wouldn't he just have finished what he'd started?

What he'd started at the monastery, she appended bitterly, realising that that must be where the inspiration for this repulsive dream had come from. Heaven help her, what kind of a woman was she to entertain such thoughts about a man who had already got her friend pregnant and would likely do the same to her given the chance...?

She shivered violently as she was gripped with the realisation that that was what she'd wanted, what she'd dreamed of. She'd wanted Matteo to make her pregnant. She'd wanted to have his child!

Her throat constricted, and she flung herself out of bed, only to stare aghast at her naked body. As well as tearing her hair out of its braid, she must also have torn off her tee shirt. It lay where she had flung it, at the end of the bed, and she snatched it up with shaking hands and put it on before wrapping her arms tightly about herself.

Dear God, was she going out of her mind? What mad attraction did Matteo di Falco exert that turned a normally sane and sensible young woman into a raving lunatic? Whatever it was, the sooner she escaped from its clutches the better.

By the time she'd taken a long shower, she was begin-

ning to feel a little more human. She'd run the tap hot at
first, allowing its stinging needles to burn all sensitivity
from her skin, before turning off the heat altogether. Ice-
cold water was a great energiser, but she was shivering
when she stepped out of the shower cubicle onto the cool
marble tiles.

She dried herself on one of the huge bath sheets. She
deliberately avoided looking at her reflection as she shed
the towel and wrapped herself in the enveloping folds of a
soft bathrobe. She had no desire to see the guilt she knew
must be there in her face, and she spent the time between
then and going down to breakfast in drying her hair and
packing the few belongings she'd brought with her. Not for
the first time, she wished she had her own transport, but
she owed it to the *marchesa* to behave as if nothing had
happened.

And it hadn't, she reminded herself painfully. Indeed,
until she'd awakened that morning, she'd been congratu-
lating herself on avoiding the possible outcome of her own
foolishness. Everything could have gone so wrong, but
somehow she'd succeeded in keeping Matteo away from
her, and she'd gone to bed the previous evening feeling as
if what had happened at the monastery had just been a
momentary aberration on her part.

No longer.

Now she knew the depths of her own depravity, and
nothing she did now could remove the stigma of treachery
from her. She'd betrayed Julia—not actually, but in every
way that mattered to her, and she could never forgive herself for that. She could blame Matteo as much as she liked,
but nothing would have happened, either at the monastery
or in her dreams, if she hadn't willed it. She'd wanted him
to kiss her at Sant' Emilio, and last night…

God, she didn't even want to speculate about what she'd
wanted from him last night. Even thinking of it now could
still bring a wave of uncontrollable longing sweeping over

her, and she groaned aloud at the realisation that she was
beyond redemption.

It was a foolish idea, but she chose to wear her least
flattering outfit to go down to breakfast. Black leggings and
a thigh-length cotton tee shirt showed a lack of concern for
her appearance that she didn't often display. Let Julia daz-
zle her host, she thought, in one of the many outfits she
had that showed her cleavage. She would look drab and
ungainly, while Julia would be her petite, provocative self.

Grace delayed going downstairs until Julia came to find
her. Her friend looked infinitely brighter this morning, ex-
hibiting none of the morning sickness she'd suffered the
previous day. As Grace had expected, Julia was wearing a
sleeveless top that emphasised her small bosom, and hip-
hugging khaki trousers that drew attention to her pert behind.

'Heavens, what do you look like?' she exclaimed, viewing Grace's appearance with obvious amusement. 'Anyone
would think you were trying to put the *marchesa*'s back
up. Are you?'

'Of course not.' Grace wasn't too happy that she should
think that. Then, deciding it didn't matter to her what the
marchesa thought of her, she added, 'Anyway, let's go. I
expect we'll be starting back after breakfast.'

'Not immediately after,' protested Julia as they walked
along the corridor. 'I'm hoping Matt will spend some time
with me this morning. I feel as though I wasted yesterday.'

'But—you did spend time with him last night, didn't
you?' Grace ventured carefully. 'I mean, after I'd gone to
bed?'

'No.' Julia pulled a face. 'Would you believe it, Ceci
had him take her to some party at a villa in the next valley,
and I wasn't even up when he got back?'

'No?'

'Yes.' Julia grimaced. 'I hung on as long as I could, but
it was obvious that the old lady wasn't going to let me wait

alone, and if he had come back sooner she'd have probably
devised some new task for him to do.'

Grace hated the way her heart leapt at the realisation that
Matteo hadn't spent the night in Julia's bed, and she hurried
into offering an alternative strategy. 'Look,' she said, 'why
don't I make some excuse about wanting to get back this
morning? The chauffeur can drive me, and later on—this
afternoon or this evening; that's up to you—Matteo can
bring you home.'

Julia frowned, but it was obvious that the idea appealed
to her. 'We could do that, couldn't we?' she agreed, her
excitement building. She squeezed Grace's arm. 'You don't
mind?'

'Not at all.'

Grace was appalled at her own duplicity, but she was
glad she had suggested it when they stepped out into the
loggia to find Matteo and his grandmother sharing a pot of
coffee.

Anything to avoid spending any more time with Matteo
than she had to, she thought grimly as he came politely to
his feet, and then wanted to die of embarrassment when his
dark eyes moved appraisingly over her shapeless tee shirt
and the unsuitable leggings beneath. She could almost tell
what he was thinking, and, avoiding a confrontation, she
went to greet the *marchesa*.

She was aware of Matteo exchanging a few stilted words
with Julia as she spoke to the old lady, and then he was at
her side, his intentions obvious. 'Sleep well?' he asked
softly, taking the incredible liberty of tucking an unruly
strand of newly washed hair behind her ear. 'You look—
unrested.'

'Tired, do you mean?' She rounded on him and then
attempted to retrieve her composure when she found both
Julia and the *marchesa* watching their exchange with evident interest. 'I—didn't sleep very well.'

'Nor did I,' he told her, with blatant familiarity in his
gaze, and she stared at him in sudden confusion.

Just for a moment, his words reminded her of the dangerous intimacy they'd shared in her dream, and she swayed a little as she dragged her eyes away from his. Dear God, she thought weakly, she had to get away from here before she betrayed her feelings to Julia as well as herself.

It was the *marchesa* who saved her. As if sensing the sudden tension between them, she intervened with a comment of her own, although what she had to say was no more welcome to Grace's peace of mind than her grandson's presumption had been earlier.

'Matteo has made a suggestion to me, Grace,' she declared pleasantly, ignoring Julia completely after their initial greeting. 'It had occurred to me, too, and in the circumstances I think it's an excellent idea. The suggestion is that you should stay on here for the next few days. Staying in a small apartment is all very well, but you'd have far more room here at the villa and the atmosphere is much more restful.'

More restful? With Matteo watching her every move? thought Grace wildly. Oh, yes! About as restful as a mongoose in a pit full of snakes!

She was about to make the excuse that she had to go back to England sooner than she'd expected, when Julia broke in.

'Grace is eager to get back to Portofalco, Marchesa,' she said swiftly. 'Why, she was just telling me this morning that there's nothing to do here. She wants to leave straight after breakfast, don't you, Grace? That is what you said, isn't it?'

Grace pressed her lips together. 'I did say that, yes,' she murmured, but the heat that flowered in her cheeks wasn't just an indication of her embarrassment. She was angry, too; angry that Julia should use her to gain the *marchesa*'s approval.

'Oh, well—'

The *marchesa*'s nostrils flared briefly, but her grandson was not about to let Julia have it all her own way. 'I'm

sure Grace was only saying what she knew Julia wanted to
hear, Nonna,' he essayed smoothly, and when Julia would
have protested he silenced her with a look. 'We all know
that you find staying at the villa boring,' he added, with a
Latin shrug of his shoulders. 'Naturally I'll have Gianni
take you back to Portofalco this morning.'

'No!'

Julia was horrified, but not more so than Grace herself.
'Really,' she said, 'it's very kind of you to invite me to
stay on, Marchesa, but I do have to get back to England.'

'Why?'

It was Matteo who asked the question, but it was obvious
that his grandmother was waiting for an answer, too, and
Grace's mind buzzed as she sought for a convincing reply.

'Does it matter?' Once again, it was Julia who spoke.
'And you're wrong: I love staying at the villa, whatever
Matt says, Marchesa. And I'm sure if I had a word with
my manager at the hotel he'd be happy for me to stay on
for another couple of days.'

'You misunderstand me, Miss Calloway.' The old lady
was at her most daunting. 'I didn't invite you to prolong
your stay. The invitation was for Grace, and Grace alone.'

Julia couldn't have looked more shocked if she'd tried,
and when Matteo seconded his grandmother's words all
Grace wanted was for the floor to open up and swallow
her. 'Stay, *cara*,' he murmured huskily. 'Please, Grace. For
me.'

Julia's expression altered. In the space of a moment it
changed from outrage to suspicion to bitter disbelief. And
Grace couldn't blame her. Dear God, she'd never dreamt
that Matteo might use what had happened at the monastery
against Julia, that he'd reveal their despicable intimacy as
a means of showing the other woman that she was wasting
her time in pursuing their relationship. And especially not
when his grandmother was looking on and listening to
every word.

Julia's strangled, 'What is this?' broke the awful silence that had fallen, and Grace turned to her with desperate eyes.

'It's all a mistake,' she began weakly, but Matteo wasn't having that.

'It's no mistake,' he said, his normally relaxed features drawn into a severe mask. 'I asked Nonna to invite Grace to stay on so that we could have more time to get to know one another.'

'To get to know one another?' Julia looked from him to Grace and back again. 'What the hell is that supposed to mean?'

'What do you think it means?' Matteo asked impatiently. 'Do you need me to spell it out for you?'

'Oh, please—'

Grace tried to intervene, but Julia wasn't listening to her. 'Yes, I think I do,' she said harshly. 'I think I need to know what you intend to do when it was me and not Grace that you invited here.'

'Julia—'

Once again, Grace tried to get a word in, but before she could say anything more she became aware of the *marchesa* at her elbow.

'Leave them, child,' she advised, her patrician features as severe when she looked at Julia as her grandson's. 'This has been a long time in coming.'

'And what would you know about it?' demanded Julia suddenly, proving that she was not unaware of the other people in the room. She turned to Matteo's grandmother with a venomous expression on her pale face. 'Do you honestly think you can get rid of me as easily as this?'

'Miss Calloway—'

'Julia!'

The *marchesa* and her grandson spoke at once, but Julia wouldn't be silenced and Grace could hardly blame her. This was all her fault, she thought guiltily. If she'd never let Julia talk her into coming here, none of this would have happened. Who knew? Given time Julia and Matteo's relationship might have deepened, whereas now...

The uneasy suspicion occurred to her that perhaps she had been just a pawn in a rather cruel game. What if Matteo's supposed attraction to her had been manufactured as a way to prove to Julia that she was just wasting her time with him? The *marchesa* had been kind, it was true, but Grace had the feeling that the old lady would do anything to protect her grandson, to protect her whole family...

'You don't understand,' Julia said thickly now. 'Grace does, but she's apparently forgotten what I told her.'

'Julia, please—'

Grace's eyes implored her friend not to do this, not right now, not in such a confrontational way, but once again Julia ignored her.

'I'd have thought you might have had a suspicion yesterday,' she went on maliciously. 'Morning sickness, and all that. But perhaps it's so long since there's been a baby in the family that you've forgotten the symptoms!'

'*A baby!*'

It was the *marchesa* who echoed her words, who groped unsteadily for the chair where she had been sitting before their arrival and sank down weakly onto the cushions. No one else moved or said anything, and Grace watched the old lady struggling to gather the shreds of her dignity about her before whispering hoarsely, 'Matteo, tell me it's not true!'

But Matteo couldn't tell her any such thing. Grace could see that he had been as stunned by Julia's announcement as the *marchesa*, but he had the knowledge of his own intimate involvement with her to prevent an automatic denial.

'Is it true?' he asked instead, turning to Grace and not Julia, and although she knew it shouldn't matter to her she shared his raw frustration.

She nodded. 'Yes...'

'You knew?' His eyes tormented her. 'And you didn't tell me?'

'I asked her not to,' said Julia smugly. She savoured the moment. 'I wanted the pleasure of telling you myself, darling. Aren't you thrilled? I am.' She cast a disparaging look at his grandmother. 'I've always wanted to have a family of my own.'

CHAPTER ELEVEN

IT WAS late in the evening when Grace got back to Brighton, and by then she was utterly exhausted. It had been an exhausting day, not just physically but mentally, and all she wanted to do was fall into bed and find a total escape in oblivion.

Running away had been an escape of sorts, of course, but the physical removal of herself from the nightmare events in Italy just didn't cut it. She was still there in spirit, and she thought she would never forget the look on Matteo's face when she told him she was leaving.

Not that he had had much chance to express his real feelings, whatever they might be. Apart from the fact that he had still seemed to be dazed by Julia's revelation, Julia herself had made sure that they were never left alone together.

Soon after Julia's announcement, the *marchesa* had retired to her own apartments, and Grace could only imagine the effect this news might have on the old lady. She had never struck Grace as being frail until that morning, but when one of the footmen had assisted her out of the room she had looked incredibly fragile.

Which made her own role in the proceedings even more unforgivable. Whatever plans Matteo might have had for her, whether indeed he had had any real interest in her or not, didn't matter now. She had conspired with Julia to deceive the whole di Falco family, and, whatever the outcome, she was not wanted there.

That was when she had remembered the name of the taxi firm in Portofalco. She'd seen the cabs buzzing about the town with their distinctive logo flashing like a beacon on the roofs of the vehicles, and it had been such a relief to be able to do something for herself. She'd known Matteo would have arranged for the chauffeur to take her back to the apartment if she'd asked him, but she'd wanted nothing more to do with the grim-faced master of the villa. Besides, she'd preferred Julia not to know what she was planning until it was too late to do anything about it.

It had been a simple matter to make the call from her room, and then she'd hung about there until a suitable interval had elapsed and she could be sure the taxi was well on its way.

Her bags were already packed, so it had been a simple matter to transport them to the front of the villa. She'd seen no one but members of the *marchesa*'s staff as she'd traversed the now familiar corridors, but when she'd emerged onto the terrace she had not been so lucky. Matteo had been there, and Julia, and he'd stared blankly at the bags in her hands.

'What's going on?'

'I'm leaving.' Grace had thought it was obvious. 'I've—called a cab. It'll be here soon.'

'A cab!'

Matteo had looked stunned, but Julia had had no such reservations. 'It's probably for the best,' she'd declared, with a careless shrug. 'Grace knows that we've got things to talk about, plans to make. Don't embarrass her by making her feel any worse than she already does.'

Grace didn't know what Matteo might have had to say to that because the taxi had arrived at that moment, proving she had estimated its journey time with more accuracy than she'd shown about anything else.

But he had insisted on carrying her bags down the terrace steps and stowing them in the taxi's boot for her. 'This isn't a good idea,' he'd said finally, when she would have brushed past him to get into the back of the cab. 'Grace, I mean it. This isn't the end.'

'It is for me,' Grace had mumbled, not trusting herself

to look at him, and, as if sensing a conspiracy, Julia had come down the steps to join them.

'I'll see you back at the apartment,' she'd said, for all the world as if nothing momentous had occurred, and Grace hadn't disillusioned her. But when she'd looked back at them, standing at the foot of the steps as the taxi drove away, she'd wanted to weep at the devastation she'd seen in Matteo's face.

She'd asked the taxi to wait while she collected the rest of her belongings from the apartment in Portofalco, somehow managing to make Benito understand that she wouldn't be coming back. The old caretaker had looked positively disappointed, too, when she'd driven away, and she'd known that whatever happened in the future she would never forget the people she'd met here.

She was lucky enough to get a seat on a flight leaving Pisa in the late afternoon, and she'd arrived at Heathrow in the early evening with an odd feeling of disorientation. It was familiar, yet not familiar somehow, and she'd realised it wasn't the airport that had changed, it was herself.

She'd had to take the tube into London to make a connection to Brighton, and by the time she'd suffered a diversion, due to a problem with the signalling system, Grace was in no mood to be sociable. She was looking forward to getting home and going straight to bed. Her mother, she knew, generally retired early, and she was hoping to avoid any explanations until the morning. She would have to tell her mother what had happened, of course, but not tonight.

However, when the taxi dropped her outside her mother's modest semi in Islington Crescent, she saw at once that there were lights burning in several windows, upstairs and down, and that her brother-in-law's Mondeo was parked in the driveway.

Her heart skipped a beat. Surely nothing had happened to her mother? she fretted, hauling her bags up the path to the front door and fumbling for her key. No. She struggled to get the key in the lock as she assured herself that they would have let her know if anything was wrong, and then felt another surge of anxiety at the realisation that she hadn't been available for anyone to get in touch with all today.

Her key turned, but the door didn't open, and she uttered a minor expletive as she took it out and examined it for identification purposes. But no, it was the right key, and she realized that someone must have slipped the bolt, too. She was about to try again, when the door was suddenly opened to her, and her nine-year-old niece gazed delightedly up at her.

'Aunty Grace!' she exclaimed. 'What are you doing here? I thought you were on holiday in Italy.'

Grace forced a smile. 'I was,' she said, looking over Sharon's head to where her sister was standing in the dining-room doorway. 'What's going on? Mum's not—'

'Nanna's fine,' said Sharon at once, before her mother could reply. 'We've come to live with her.'

'What?'

Grace couldn't prevent the astonished exclamation, and her sister gave her daughter an impatient look. 'Go into the living room and see if Daddy wants any more coffee,' she directed Sharon shortly. 'Hurry up, now. I want to talk to Aunty Grace.'

Grace bet she did. Blinking a little in the hall light, she dragged her suitcase over the threshold, and, closing the front door, leaned back against it. 'I asked, what's going on?'

'I know that.' Pauline folded her arms rather protectively across her midriff. Unlike her sister, she was dark and rather sallow-complexioned, and it had pleased her no end when she'd beaten Grace to the altar. 'I could ask you the same thing.'

'Yes. Well...' Grace didn't want to get into that; not yet. 'We'll come to me in a minute. What did Sharon mean about you moving in?'

Pauline sighed. 'She shouldn't have said anything.

Nothing's been decided yet. But I can't deny that we—that is, Mum and Giles and I—have been discussing it.'

Grace shook her head. She was beginning to feel the way Alice must have felt when she fell down the rabbit hole. Nothing seemed to make sense any more.

'But why?' she asked, feeling dazed. 'I was only planning on being away for a couple of weeks.'

'Oh, I know that,' said Pauline airily, 'but you've always said how difficult it was for you holding down two jobs at the same time.'

'I haven't—'

'Well, Mum has, then. She's always saying how busy you always are. Too busy to baby-sit, even, if you remember?'

Grace blinked. This couldn't all have come about because she'd refused to baby-sit the last time Pauline asked her, could it?

'All the same...'

'Look, Grace—' Pauline gestured towards the living room, where they could hear the television playing at full blast '—go and sit down. I'll bring you a cup of tea. Then we can talk about things in comfort.'

Grace didn't move. 'Where's Mum?'

'Where she always is at this hour of the evening,' replied Pauline, with a sniff. 'She's in bed, of course. But if you go up to see her, don't wake Hannah, will you? I've just got her off.'

Hannah was Pauline's younger child. An afterthought, Mrs Horton called her, and it was true there were seven years between Sharon and her baby sister.

Grace endeavoured not to reveal her own feelings at this news and, picking up her case again, she started up the stairs. Perhaps her mother would be able to explain why, just over a week after she'd left England, her sister and her family had decided to take up residence in the family home.

Mrs Horton looked up from her book in some surprise when her eldest daughter let herself into her bedroom.

'Grace,' she said, and Grace was relieved to see that at least her mother had the decency to look a little guilty. 'What are you doing here?'

'I live here,' said Grace shortly, and then, guessing this hadn't been her mother's idea, she sank down wearily onto the side of the bed. 'So—' she put their other problems aside for the moment '—how are you?'

'Oh—not too bad.' Mrs Horton managed a faint smile. 'I manage. How about you? You're looking a little better, I must say.'

'Thanks.' Grace was amazed that that was true. 'I'm okay. Change of plans, that's all.'

Mrs Horton shook her head. 'You should have let us know.'

'Yeah, right.' Grace was sardonic. 'Tell me about it.'

'Well—'

'No—' Grace reached out and clasped one of her mother's hands, stroking the swollen knuckles with genuine contrition. 'That's just an expression. I didn't mean it as it sounded.'

'Nevertheless, you deserve to know,' declared Mrs Horton, gazing at her eldest daughter with troubled eyes. 'It's Giles, you see. He's lost his job—again.'

Grace groaned. 'Not again.'

'I'm afraid so.' Her mother sighed. 'There was some money missing from the petty cash, you see, and although he swears it was nothing to do with him someone saw him at the race track last week, and so—'

She broke off but Grace understood only too well. Her brother-in-law was an inveterate gambler, and it wasn't the first time her mother had had to use what little money her husband had left her to bail him out.

'But why did Sharon say they were moving in here?' she asked gently. 'Is that your decision?'

'Well, it does seem a possible solution,' agreed Mrs Horton reluctantly. 'There's no way Pauline can continue to pay the mortgage on their house with no money coming in.'

'But he'll get another job, won't he?'

'I hope so. He certainly seems to have learnt his lesson this time. I suppose it depends what happens when the case goes to court,' said Mrs Horton, looking down at their clasped hands, and Grace groaned.

'It's not going to court, surely?'

'Well, it might,' admitted her mother unhappily. 'And until then I couldn't let those two children go without, could I?'

'No.' Grace conceded the point. She knew her mother thought the world of her grandchildren, and she could hardly blame her because she was doing what she thought was best for all of them. 'So,' she added softly, 'where does that leave me?'

'That's up to you,' said Mrs Horton at once. 'This is your home, and if you want to stay here, then of course you must. But—' she hesitated '—it hasn't escaped my notice that one of the reasons you were so susceptible to that illness you had was because you've been trying to do too much. Travelling up and down to London every day, working at the museum, serving part-time behind the bar at the Royal Oak, trying to keep everybody happy—it's too much.'

Grace looked doubtful. 'So what's your solution?'

'Oh, I don't know...' Mrs Horton looked embarrassed now. 'I can't make your decisions for you, Grace. But it seems to me you were a long way happier when you had your own place in town.'

Grace expelled an unsteady breath. She'd known where this was heading, of course, from the minute Sharon had blurted the news that she and her parents had moved in. The ironic thing was, before she'd gone away, she'd have probably welcomed the idea. Now, however, all she wanted to do was bury herself in the bosom of her family. She'd even been considering giving up her job at the museum and trying to find something suitable nearer home, but it appeared she wasn't going to be given the opportunity. There was no way she could live here with Pauline and her family, and they both knew it. For one thing, she and Giles had never hit it off, and the knowledge that he'd been lying to her sister yet again could only sour the situation even more.

'Oh, Grace—'

Her mother was looking really worried now, and Grace knew she couldn't allow her to know what she was thinking. 'You could be right,' she said, with determined brightness. 'Yes, I think it might prove advantageous all round.'

After all, she thought, Pauline loved their mother too. Why did she always think she was the only support her mother had?

'Are you sure?' Mrs Horton wasn't yet convinced. Then another thought occurred to her. 'You still haven't told me what you're doing home. Is Julia all right?'

Grace knew a hysterical desire to laugh. 'Oh, yes,' she said. 'Julia's all right.' But she couldn't bring herself to tell her mother about the baby. 'I just—got bored, that's all. There's not a lot to do in Portofalco.'

Two weeks later, Grace moved into a rented apartment in St John's Wood.

Despite her initial misgivings, the move had proved beneficial in the end. It had given her something to do, something to think about, other than her emotional problems. And, although her world had still not yet settled back onto its axis, finding the apartment and furnishing it had provided her with an alternative to the chaos of her thoughts.

The curator at the museum had been pleased to see her, too, although he had insisted she give herself another couple of weeks before returning to work.

'We don't want you having a relapse because you haven't given yourself time to recover, do we?' he asked, his curiously youthful features mirroring a very genuine concern. And, even though Grace knew he had to be at least sixty, as usual he behaved as if she was much older than himself.

And, goodness knew, she felt it, she mused as the prospect of spending another two weeks browsing round the shops or visiting her mother filled her with apprehension. She had hoped that getting back to work would restore her stability, but now it seemed she was to suffer her anguish a little longer.

In Brighton, Pauline and Giles had now settled into the house in Islington Crescent, and Pauline was even talking of getting a job herself if she could get Hannah into a crèche. Even Giles had thanked Grace for moving out. Although he'd spoiled it afterwards by suggesting that living with her mother must have cramped her style.

When would people—men, in particular—ever get it into their heads that she wanted more out of life than promiscuous sex? Grace wondered wearily. It was as if she went around with a sign on her head. All she'd ever wanted was someone to love her for herself.

She hadn't heard a word from Julia since her return, but that hadn't surprised her. If she knew Julia, she'd be too busy preparing for her coming nuptials to care what had happened to her erstwhile friend. Although she didn't know all the details, she must have guessed what had been going on between Grace and Matteo, and she had every right to feel aggrieved that Grace should have betrayed her in that way.

As far as Matteo was concerned, Grace had to concede that Julia did have a different agenda. Despite the way he'd deceived her, she was evidently prepared to forgive him to gain her own ends. But Grace couldn't help wondering if love had ever come into it, for either of them. Matteo had insisted it hadn't, and she was very much afraid he was right.

Not that that excused his behaviour, she told herself doggedly. However tempted she might be to feel sorry for him, she mustn't forget he'd brought it on himself. But oh—her lips trembled—she couldn't forget how he'd made her feel. After everything that had happened, she was still a sucker for love…

She spent the Sunday before she was due to start back at the museum sorting out some of the boxes she'd brought up from Brighton the previous day. They were full of books and papers she'd been storing since her university days, and she'd been promising herself that she'd get rid of them for ages.

She wasted some time reading over old essays she'd written and pulling faces at faded photographs that revealed what an innocent she'd been then. It was almost painful to remember the dreams she'd had when she was eighteen, when the whole of her life had seemed to be ahead of her. Now, she felt as if the better part of it was behind her, and the emotional torment she'd suffered these past weeks had seemed to prove it.

She came across a picture of herself and Julia as students, and although she was tempted to consign it to the pile of papers she was throwing out she didn't. How young they looked, she thought, feeling a sudden wave of nostalgia. She sighed. Poor Julia. It wasn't her fault that Grace had fallen in love with the man she wanted to marry. But what chance of happiness would she have with a man like Matteo di Falco? Marriage had never been on his agenda, and would his wealth really make up for what she was giving up?

It wasn't something Grace wanted to think about, and, stowing the photograph in the bottom of the box that contained the things she was going to keep, she picked it up and carried it into the bedroom.

One of the disadvantages of the small apartment was its lack of cupboard space, and she was standing with her hands on her hips, studying the possibility of stowing boxes in the wardrobe, when the doorbell rang.

She sighed. Now who was that? As far as she was aware, only the members of her own family knew this address, except Mr Seton, of course, and he was unlikely to spread it around. No. The most likely solution was that it was Karen and her husband come to view her new home. Ever since Pauline and her husband had moved back into their mother's house, Karen had taken every opportunity to grumble about her, but Grace had so far avoided getting involved in family politics. If Karen resented the fact that she and her family were stuck in a small town house while Pauline's children had the run of Islington Crescent, that was her problem. Grace didn't have an opinion.

Smoothing her ink-stained fingers down the seams of her old jeans, she prepared herself for yet another family argument. She looked a mess, she thought, catching a glimpse of herself in the mirror she had hung in the tiny hallway, but she hadn't been expecting company and she had no intention of wearing good clothes to clear out dusty old boxes. Nevertheless, she had to admit that the cropped tee shirt had seen better days, and Karen's husband, Dave, would probably have some sarcastic comment to make.

'All right, all right,' she muttered as the bell rang again, and, releasing the safety chain, she opened the door. 'I was in the other—'

'Ciao, cara.'

Grace broke off what she was saying in total confusion. At no time had she ever believed she would see Matteo di Falco again—except maybe on a wedding photograph, if Julia relented enough to send her one—and she could only stare at him with wide, uncomprehending eyes.

'May I come in?'

He looked beyond her, through the door into the living room, and, glancing behind her, she saw what he could see: boxes and books, and papers still strewn all over the floor.

'I—what are you doing here?' she asked, tugging the tee shirt over her bare midriff as several explanations, none of them admirable, tumbled through her shocked mind. Did

Julia know he was here, or didn't she? Were they still to-gether, or—God help her!—had they parted, and if so what did that mean to her?

Matteo propped his shoulder against the jamb. It was the first time she'd seen him in a suit, and the fine dark blue fabric fitted his lean, athletic frame with loving dexterity. He looked—fantastic, she thought foolishly. And much more Italian in these essentially English surroundings.

'How are you?' he asked, not answering her question, and she wondered if it was only wish-fulfilment on her part that made her think there was a certain weary hollowness around his eyes.

'I'm all right,' she said quickly. 'Um—is Julia with you?'

Matteo's eyes grew sardonic. 'Does it look like it?' he asked, glancing up and down the landing, but she refused to let him disconcert her.

'Why not?' she asked defensively. 'Unless—' Her mouth felt as dry as old boots. 'Unless you're not together any longer; unless you're not getting married, after all.'

Matteo straightened. 'Oh—we are still together, *cara*,' he told her in a tired voice, thereby dashing all the pitiful hopes she'd been trying to discipline ever since she'd opened the door. 'Julia is arranging the wedding, even as we speak.' He blew out a breath. 'Please let me come in. We have to talk.'

Grace stiffened. 'I don't think we have anything to say to one another—'

'You're wrong.'

He didn't move, and, telling herself she didn't want her new neighbours to think she was in the habit of entertaining men on the doorstep, she moved out of his way. This might be the very last chance she had of telling him what she thought of him, she defended herself as common sense derided her weakness, and, closing the door behind her, she followed him into the living room.

'You're not living with your mother,' he said, looking

around, and she remembered that she hadn't given him her address.

'How did you know?' she asked tautly, and Matteo's mouth compressed.

'Because I drove down to Brighton myself this morning,' he told her briefly. 'Fortunately, Julia had told me some weeks ago where you worked, and the receptionist at the museum was very...kind.' As she was absorbing this astonishing news he asked, 'Do you have anything to drink?'

Grace glanced towards the tiny kitchenette. 'I've got tea or coffee,' she said, wondering what Pauline and her mother must be thinking. 'I don't have wine, if that's what you mean.'

'Coke will do. Or beer.' His voice was flat. 'I'm thirsty, that's all. It's hot out, or hadn't you noticed?'

Grace was once again reminded of the skimpiness of her top, but she refused to let him see that he'd embarrassed her as she walked into the kitchen. He'd seen her breasts, for God's sake! Though that didn't help much either.

She came back with a can of Coke to find him sitting on the worn leather sofa she'd bought second-hand. He wasn't immediately aware of her return, and she was ashamed to admit that the weary slope of his shoulders disturbed her. His head was bent, his hands hanging loosely between his spread thighs, and just for a moment he looked totally vulnerable.

But that was stupid, she told herself crossly, even as her heart went out to him. He wasn't going to inspire her sympathy no matter what he did, and she was a fool for letting him in here in the first place.

'Here you are.'

She held the can and a glass out to him, thereby removing any pathos from the situation, but he only took the can from her. He flipped the tab and raised it to his lips, the muscles in his throat moving rhythmically as he swallowed. Then, panting a little, he licked a curl of foam from his upper lip before saying, 'Thanks.'

Grace shrugged, making no response, and, deciding she couldn't go on towering over him, she subsided onto an upholstered chair at the other side of the room. She thought a faint look of self-mockery crossed his face at this rather obvious separation, but he finished his Coke before going on.

'I spoke to your mother,' he said, returning to the subject of her changed circumstances. 'She said you'd moved back to London.'

'Did she?' Grace nodded. 'Well, as you can see, I have.'

'Did something go wrong at home?' he asked, and although she told herself it was nothing to do with him she found herself explaining that her sister's husband had lost his job, and that it was obviously easier for them if they didn't have a household's bills to pay.

'This would be—Giles, am I right?' he enquired, and she acknowledged that very little escaped his attention.

'Giles, that's right. He used to work for an insurance company in Brighton.'

'And what happened? Were they downsizing, or what?'

Grace thought how crazy it was that they should be discussing her brother-in-law, but it was easier than talking about the real reason Matteo was here.

'My brother-in-law likes—gambling,' she conceded after a moment. 'Unfortunately, he can't always afford to do so.'

'I see.' Matteo nodded, and she was quite sure he knew exactly what she was talking about. 'So he was fired.'

'That's right.' Grace sighed, and then muttered barely audibly, 'If only that was all.'

'So he is to be—charged with—what? Embezzlement?'

'Something like that.' Grace felt as if she'd said more than enough. She squared her shoulders. 'But that isn't why you came, is it?'

'No.' He subjected her to the kind of intent appraisal that had always been able to turn her knees to water. 'I had to see you again.'

'Oh, please—'

Grace's hands came to grip the edge of her seat in an instinctive preliminary to flight, and he spread his hands in a desperate gesture. 'Listen to me,' he begged. And then, as if realising he was still holding the empty can, he crushed it with savage fingers and tossed it onto the coffee table between them. 'You have to know,' he went on in a harsh voice. 'I did—*I do*—care about you—'

Grace sprang to her feet. 'I think you'd better go.'

'Why?' He got to his feet, too, and although there was at least eight feet between them Grace was sure she could feel his frustration. 'I'm not suggesting I abandon my responsibilities to Julia. God knows, if she is expecting my child, then naturally I owe her my name and my support.' He paused for a moment, as if to calm himself, and then went on, 'Nonna told me that she'd explained to you about the way Luisa died, so I know you'll understand when I say that I would not have been thrilled about her condition in any circumstances, but be assured she will have the best of care.'

Grace nodded. 'I never doubted it.'

'No.' Matteo's lips twisted. 'No, you didn't, did you? From the very beginning of our association, you tried to tell me that I was wasting my time, but I didn't want to listen.'

Grace swallowed. 'Julia should have told you sooner.'

'Yes, she should.' Matteo conceded the point. 'She should have trusted in the fact that we are Roman Catholics. We do not believe in taking the life of an unborn child, however inconvenient its existence might be.'

Grace looked down at her hands. 'I'm sorry.'

'Why are you sorry?' Matteo took an involuntary step towards her and then halted when he saw the apprehension in her face. 'Oh, Grace, this whole sorry mess is my fault. Mine! You have nothing to reproach yourself for. Be thankful you can forget it, move on with your life, find someone else who will not bring the pitiful baggage of a weekend's madness to destroy your future—'

'Don't.' Grace couldn't bear it. She had thought she could handle this, but she couldn't. Watching him visibly destroying himself just tore her up and she couldn't let him go on. 'It was as much my fault as yours,' she told him doggedly. 'I knew—I knew about the pregnancy all along, but I still—I still—'

'What? What?'

Matteo was waiting for her answer with an anguished expression, and Grace had to steel herself against the urge she had to go and comfort him. 'I—I still wanted you,' she confessed helplessly, and heard the agonised moan that escaped his lips.

'*Dio*, Grace,' he said, his voice ragged with emotion. 'What have I done?'

Grace turned away. 'It doesn't matter—'

'Don't say that.'

He was behind her now. She could feel the draught of his breath against her neck, and she expected any moment for his hands to descend on her shoulders and for him to turn her towards him. She didn't know what she'd do when that happened; she hadn't got that far in her reasoning, but—

A door slammed.

The thud echoed in her head long after the sound had died away, and her shoulders began to shake as the tears she'd been fighting for weeks streamed down her cheeks. She didn't need to look round to know he'd gone. Something, some extra sensitivity they shared, was gone, and she knew it wasn't coming back...

CHAPTER TWELVE

IN THE weeks that followed, Grace did her best to put her life back together.

She was glad to be able to give up working at the pub, but now she applied herself to her job at the museum with renewed enthusiasm. Keeping busy was the only way she knew to keep her personal demons at bay, and she was seldom home before seven o'clock.

She also started accepting the odd social invitation that came her way. It used to be rare indeed that she attended the theatre or the opera with a male companion, but she'd decided that dating was all part of her emotional convalescence. And, if no one actually got across the threshold of her St John's Wood apartment, it wasn't through want of trying.

But it was a hollow existence. She knew she was only fooling herself by thinking that anything—or anyone— could banish Matteo from her life. He was there; he was a fixture; and everything else was just a passing diversion.

The only person who came close to discovering the truth was her mother. All Grace's family had been curious about the sexy Italian who had come to the house in Islington Crescent looking for her, but only Mrs Horton had guessed that Grace's flippant dismissal of his appearance was just an act.

'Are you in love with him?' she asked frankly, a couple of weeks after Matteo's visit when Grace had driven down to see her. She frowned. 'What is it? Is he married?'

'He probably is by now,' replied Grace with assumed brightness, but her mother wasn't letting her get away with that.

'Did he—hurt you?'

'Not intentionally,' said Grace, deciding she had to put an end to all these questions before she broke down completely. 'Now—' she got out of her chair '—I'm going to make us both a nice cup of tea, and then you can tell me how things are working out with Pauline and Giles.' She managed a conspiratorial wink. 'Before they get back from Giles's parents', eh?'

'Well, that was the funniest thing!' exclaimed Mrs Horton before she could get out of the room, and Grace was forced to pause by the door to hear the latest gossip. 'The firm have decided not to bring any charges. Against Giles, I mean, of course. It took us all by surprise when the letter arrived. You can imagine what Giles thought when he saw the company logo on the envelope.'

'I bet.' Grace frowned. 'Did they say why?'

Mrs Horton said, 'I can't remember the exact wording, but it was something to the effect that as all monies had been recovered there'd be no further action taken.'

'All monies recovered?' echoed Grace blankly. 'What does that mean? He didn't take the money in the first place?'

'No. That's not in question.' Her mother regarded her with mild impatience. 'It appears that someone has paid the money back.'

'Who? Giles?'

'No. How could he?' Mrs Horton pulled a face. 'He's got no money, has he? Well, not enough to pay back what he owed anyway.'

Grace frowned. 'So what are you saying? That you've paid it off for him?'

'No!' Mrs Horton clicked her tongue. 'Weren't you listening to me? Didn't I say it was totally unexpected? For all of us.'

Grace shook her head, and, leaving her mother to marvel anew at her son-in-law's good fortune, she went into the kitchen and plugged in the electric kettle. Well, she thought ruefully, at least it would make things easier for Pauline and the children. And maybe for Giles, too, when he tried to get another job. At least he wouldn't have the handicap of a possible conviction hanging over his head.

It was towards the end of the following week when Grace had an unexpected visitor at the museum.

She was in the basement, unpacking a box of ceramics which had just arrived from their warehouse in Purfleet, when Mr Seton himself came to tell her there was someone asking to see her in Reception.

Grace had been kneeling on the floor, but now she got to her feet, dusting off her hands as she pondered the fact that the curator should have chosen to deliver the message personally. For a heart-stopping moment, she wondered if Matteo was in London and had decided to pay her a call, which might account for Mr Seton's involvement, but her boss soon disabused her of that notion.

'You might tell Miss Calloway that I do not approve of personal visitors during opening hours,' he stated brusquely as Grace hurriedly rinsed her hands at the sink. 'And particularly not when they're—' his lips showed his distaste '—intoxicated!'

But Grace had heard nothing beyond the words 'Miss Calloway'. 'Julia,' she breathed incredulously. Julia was her visitor! She could hardly believe it.

'You will tell her, won't you?' Mr Seton called after her as she preceded him out of the basement, but once again Grace wasn't listening to him. Julia? she said to herself again. *Miss* Calloway? Surely she should have been Signora di Falco by now.

She fairly ran up the stairs, only coming to a halt a couple of steps from the top when she realised she hadn't bothered to check if her hair was tidy and her face was clean. Wetting the tips of her fingers, she smoothed a few errant strands of hair behind her ears and then continued more sedately into the foyer. Julia wouldn't care what she looked like, anyway, she assured herself. She only hoped she hadn't come to make a scene.

The museum comprised several exhibition halls on three floors, with the reception area to the right of the entrance. The steps from the basement emerged immediately outside the reception hall, but Grace could hear Julia long before she pushed through the heavy glass doors. Her friend was haranguing the receptionist in a loud, demanding voice and suddenly Grace understood why Mr Seton had been so tetchy. Dear God, was Julia drunk, or was she just spoiling for a fight?

'I'm telling you, Grace will be very happy to see me,' she was proclaiming angrily as Grace pushed through the door. 'I don't care if she is working. I've come all the way from Italy to see her.'

'And here I am,' said Grace quietly, attracting the other woman's attention. 'I'm sorry about this, Sally,' she added to the young girl behind the desk. 'I came as quickly as I could.'

Julia swung round on heels that Grace was sure she wouldn't even be able to stand in, let alone walk in, and surveyed the new arrival with a jaundiced eye. 'Yes, there you are,' she said, swaying back against the desk for support. 'At last. I was beginning to think they'd buried you among all the other old artifacts.'

'And hello to you, too,' said Grace drily, noting the unmistakable cut of the designer suit her friend was wearing with an unwelcome hollowness in her stomach. Evidently Julia hadn't wasted any time in spending Matteo's money.

Julia's eyes glazed over for a moment, and Grace was very much afraid she was going to pass out. But then she seemed to pull herself together, and, leaving the security of the desk, she started across the floor.

'Come on,' she said, slinging an arm around Grace's waist, as much for support as in affection. 'Let's get out of this crappy place. I saw a little bar round the corner. I'll buy you some champagne, just for old times' sake.'

'I can't, Julia.' Grace allowed the other woman to hang onto her, but she made no move towards the door. 'It's only half-past two, and I don't finish till six, at the earliest. You can go back to my apartment and wait, if you want.'

'Your apartment?' Julia wrinkled her nose. 'Where is it? Somewhere around here?'

'It's in St John's Wood, actually,' said Grace reluctantly, 'but you could take a taxi.'

Julia shook her head, and then swayed when she almost lost her balance. 'I don't want to wait in *your* apartment,' she protested shrilly. 'I've got a suite at the Dorchester. Why don't we go there?'

'I've told you, I can't.'

'Why not? Why not?'

'You know why not,' began Grace uneasily, aware that a visitor could arrive at any moment and find her holding up an apparently drunken woman, which would not be good for the museum's reputation.

And, as if on cue, the door opened behind her. But it wasn't a visitor; it was Mr Seton. He took in the scene in a moment, and although Grace was sure she'd hear about it later he came to an immediate decision.

'Perhaps it would be as well if you escorted Miss Calloway home, Grace,' he declared, with a disparaging glance at her companion. 'We can't have—well, I think you know what I'm talking about.'

'I do, too,' put in Julia aggressively, lunging towards the curator and poking his chest with a rigid finger. 'Don't you patronise me, old man. I can buy and sell this place a dozen times over!'

'Julia—'

'I'm sure you could.' Mr Seton was not impressed, however. 'Grace! Can I leave this to you?'

'Yes, Mr Seton—'

'Yes, Mr Seton,' Julia mimicked her in a babyish voice. 'No, Mr Seton. Three bags full, Mr Seton—'

'Julia, for goodness' sake—'

Grace couldn't wait to get her out of there, and after snatching her bag and jacket from the cloakroom at the back of the reception area she ushered her friend outside.

The air, muggy though it was, seemed to knock Julia for six, and it was left to Grace to support her friend and summon a passing cab.

'She's not going to be sick, is she?' the taxi driver asked suspiciously, eyeing Julia's pale face with a wary eye, and although Grace assured him that there was no fear of that she couldn't help crossing her fingers as she did so.

'Could you take us to the Dorchester Hotel?' she asked, deciding Julia was in no state to go anywhere else. She only hoped and prayed that Matteo wasn't sharing the suite with her. She didn't know what she'd do if she had to deal with him, too.

The receptionist at the Dorchester remembered Miss Calloway very well. In no time at all, a lift had whisked them up to Julia's suite on the sixth floor, and Grace breathed a sigh of relief when the door closed behind them.

'God, I need the loo!' exclaimed Julia at once, disappearing into the bathroom, and Grace walked across to the windows and looked out on a rain-wet Park Lane. Where was Matteo? she wondered, not without some anguish. Did he have any idea how Julia was abusing her body? Abusing their unborn child?

'Haven't you helped yourself to a drink?'

Julia appeared in the doorway behind her, and Grace noticed she'd kicked off the teetering heels. She'd also shed the jacket of her suit to reveal a sleeveless silk shell and a magnificent diamond bracelet watch on her wrist.

'I'm not thirsty,' Grace said now. 'I really ought to be getting back to the museum—'

'Oh, not yet.' Julia sauntered over to the impressive wet bar and helped herself to a generous gin and tonic. Then, turning, she raised the glass to her lips. 'I bet you were surprised to see me.'

The understatement of the year, thought Grace wryly,

trying to keep her mind focussed on Julia and not on the father of the child she was carrying. 'As you say,' she murmured. Then, almost compulsively, she asked, 'Is it wise to drink so much?'

'Why not?' Julia leaned back against the bar and regarded her consideringly. 'Perhaps I need it to control the urge I have to tear your eyes out.'

'Julia—'

'Yes?'

Grace sighed and shook her head. 'I just—well, you know how sorry I am.'

'For what?' Julia arched mocking brows. 'For making love with the man I wanted to marry, even when you thought—*knew*—even when you knew I was expecting his baby?'

'We didn't—' Grace broke off, her shoulders sagging. She knew Julia would never believe they hadn't actually done 'it' so there was no point in trying to defend herself. 'I suppose so, yes.'

'You bitch!'

Grace drew a steadying breath. 'Is that what you came to say?'

'Part of it.' Julia took a generous gulp of her G and T before continuing. 'So tell me about it: how was it for you?'

Grace bent her head. 'I'd rather not discuss it!'

'I'll bet.' Julia was scornful. 'But all the same I think we should compare notes. I mean, we've got so much in common, haven't we?'

'Oh, Julia—'

'What? What?' Julia's lips curled. 'Don't give me any guff about us being such good friends. Friends don't do the dirty on one another. Friends don't pretend to be sympathetic on the one hand and jerk you off on the other.'

'I wasn't!'

'Weren't you?'

'No.' Grace spread her hands. 'You have to believe me, I never wanted to hurt you.'

'Yeah, right.' Julia swallowed another mouthful from her glass, and then wiped her wrist across her mouth, smearing her lipstick. 'No wonder I need this. You almost ruined my life.'

Grace seized on her last words. 'Only almost,' she protested. 'You've still got Matteo, haven't you?'

Julia's eyes narrowed. 'Oh, yes,' she said, after a few moments. She sneered. 'I'd forgotten about that.'

Grace didn't know how anyone could forget that they were going to be married, but perhaps it wasn't so surprising in Julia's present condition. 'So,' she said, trying to speak normally, 'where is he?' She spoke past the constriction in her throat. 'Is he in London, too?'

Julia snorted. 'Wouldn't you like to know?'

'Not particularly.' Grace was weary. 'I was just being polite.'

'Oh, polite, right.' Julia sounded sardonic. 'Always the diplomat, eh, Grace?' She finished her drink, and weighed the heavy glass in her hand. Then, dropping it carelessly onto the tray, she came towards the other woman, holding out her arm. 'What do you think of that?' she asked, indicating the watch. 'How much do you think I paid for it?'

Grace, who had had to resist the urge to back away from her, shook her head. 'I've no idea.'

'Look at it.' Julia thrust her wrist beneath Grace's nose. 'Come on; you're supposed to know about these things.'

'Not jewellery,' said Grace, wishing she'd just put Julia in a cab and let her make her own way home. 'I'm sure it was expensive.'

'You'd better believe it.' Julia examined the watch herself with jealous eyes. 'I doubt if a year's salary at that pitiful place where you work would cover it.'

'Maybe not.' Grace was trying to remain calm. 'Look— I really should be going.'

Julia's face hardened. 'It doesn't bother you, does it? You don't care about things like this.' Her chin jutted. 'You're so smug, aren't you?'

Grace's shoulders sagged. 'If you say so.'

'That's what I mean,' muttered Julia, thrusting her face close to Grace's now. 'Anyone else—anyone with *red* blood in their veins—would show a little emotion here. But not you! Goddammit, Grace, I know you're in love with him! You forget: we've known one another for a long time, and I know you.' She poked Grace in the chest as she had poked Mr Seton earlier. 'Come on, come on; admit it, damn you! You're jealous as hell that I got there first.'

Grace pushed her hand away. 'That's not true—'

'Of course it's true.' Julia was contemptuous. 'I bet it fairly burns you up, imagining us together—in bed!'

'For God's sake, Julia!' At last, the other woman had caught her on the raw, and Grace had had enough. 'Look— all right. You win. I—I am envious, yes. But that doesn't mean I don't hope that you and—and Matteo will be happy.'

'Oh, God!' Julia rocked back on her heels. 'What a hypocrite you are, Grace. You don't hope that Matt and I will be happy! It would please you no end if he and I split up.'

'No—'

Julia scowled now. 'Oh, well, have it your own way. It doesn't matter, anyway. It's not going to happen.' She spread her fingers in smug satisfaction. 'What do you think?'

Grace saw the ring then that occupied Julia's third finger. She didn't know how she could have missed it before, except that she'd been avoiding any overt curiosity, and Julia had had her hand wrapped around the glass. But now she couldn't help but stare at the huge sapphire that nestled in a circle of diamonds, and Julia twisted it round her finger, adjusting it to its best advantage.

'Impressive, huh?' she taunted. 'Bond Street's finest.'

Bond Street!

Grace stiffened. So that meant Matteo was in London, after all. Which made her desire to escape from the hotel that much more urgent.

'It's beautiful,' she said honestly, and side-stepped away from her. 'You're very lucky.'

'Aren't I, though?' But Julia's lips twisted a little mockingly as she acknowledged it.

'But I have to go,' insisted Grace again. 'Really, Julia, I do. I don't want to risk losing my job.'

'As your sister's husband did, you mean?' enquired the other woman carelessly, and Grace knew she needed no more proof that Matteo intended to go through with this marriage.

'Matteo told you,' she said, but it was not a question, and Julia preened a little in her victory.

'Of course,' she said. 'Matt tells me everything.' She grimaced. 'I didn't approve of him helping you out, but I guess I can be magnanimous in the circumstances.'

Grace flinched. 'Helping—me—out?' she said uncomprehendingly, and Julia nodded.

'Sure.' She gave a malicious little smile. 'Didn't you realise? Who did you think paid that money back that Giles had—what shall I say?—appropriated?'

Grace swallowed. 'You're not serious!'

'Why not?' Julia sauntered back to the bar to pour herself another drink. 'Matt said it was the least he could do. Recompense, I suppose, for the fool he made of you.'

CHAPTER THIRTEEN

GRACE waited several days before she decided she had to do something about what Julia had told her.

To begin with, of course, she'd wanted nothing so much as to find Matteo and tell him exactly what she thought of his 'magnanimous' gesture. But as her blood had cooled the realisation of what her anger might mean to Giles had forced her to think again. As usual, Matteo had tied her hands so tightly that there seemed little she could do to express her disgust.

She had thought, when he'd come to the apartment, that he'd had some respect for her feelings, at least. Discovering that he'd discussed her family's private problems with Julia—whatever their relationship was, he must have known how *she'd* feel about *that*—put a whole new slant on what he'd said. But that he should have done what he had to ease his conscience so far as she was concerned was totally unacceptable, and she couldn't let him get away with it.

But what could she do?

Whatever happened, she knew she couldn't risk doing anything to damage Giles's future prospects by insulting his benefactor, so she would have to find some other way of dealing with it.

And that was when she thought of the *marchesa*.

Matteo's grandmother had always been exceptionally kind to her, and although she couldn't expect her to feel quite the same about her now as she'd done before Julia's revelations she trusted the old lady would not refuse to listen to her.

But how to get in touch with her? She didn't know the

telephone number at the Villa di Falco, and something told her that it was unlikely to be freely available to just anyone who cared to ask for it. Which meant she had two choices: either she sent the *marchesa* a letter, or she must go to Italy and speak to her face to face.

Naturally, she would have preferred the former option. It would have been far easier to put what she had to say down on paper in the certain knowledge that she wouldn't be interrupted before she'd explained all the facts. But— and it was a big but—did she really want to take the chance that Julia—or someone else—might read the letter, too?

The truth was, she didn't. Indeed, she cringed at the thought that Julia might find out and think she was trying to wheedle her way back into their lives. That was the last thing she wanted to do, which meant she had to return to Italy and see the *marchesa* herself.

But not if Matteo was there, she assured herself grimly. She had no desire to see him again, particularly now, and she wondered if there was any way she could find out when Julia and the father of her child were getting married. Soon, no doubt. Matteo was a proud man. He would not want to escort a heavily pregnant bride down the aisle of the church in Valle di Falco.

But even as she was considering this another thought occurred to her. Of course. Julia and Matteo had been in London three days ago. They could still be here. Which would be ideal.

She couldn't wait to get home from work that evening and ring the Dorchester. How lucky that she knew Julia was staying there, she thought, telling herself she didn't care in the least where Matteo was staying. Just so long as he was still here, she prayed silently when the hotel receptionist answered the phone.

It was a simple matter to ask for Miss Calloway's suite, and the receptionist didn't hesitate before putting her through. Which meant Julia was still there; and where Julia went Matteo went also, Grace thought bitterly, not replacing her receiver half fast enough to prevent her hearing the pick-up. A man's voice answered, and it was not until Grace had slammed down her receiver that she had the uneasy feeling that it had not been Matteo's voice.

But, of course, it must have been, she chided herself impatiently. Who else could it be? And, in any case, she was in no state to make any kind of identification. On top of which she'd hung up so fast that his response had hardly registered.

She blew out a breath. So, there it was. Julia and Matteo were still in London, and as they said in B-movie jargon the coast was clear. All she had to do was book herself on a flight to Pisa, and hire a car to take her to the villa.

Mr Seton was not very pleased when she rang him at home later that evening to say she would not be in for the next couple of days. 'But you've just got back,' he objected irritably. 'You're not ill again, I hope.'

Grace thought about lying, and then thought better of it. 'No, I'm not ill, Mr Seton. This is—a family emergency. I'm sorry, but I have to deal with it myself.'

Mr Seton was silent for a moment and Grace could imagine the way his mouth would be compressed. 'Two days, you say?' he asked at last, and Grace hoped that it would be enough.

'Two days,' she agreed fervently, and breathed a sigh of relief when he gave her his permission.

It wasn't much easier getting a seat on a flight to Pisa. It was August now, and every flight was fully booked. It didn't help that there was a strike of French air traffic controllers, too. She eventually paid the upgrade and got a cancellation in club class, on a flight leaving at a quarter to eleven the following morning.

She phoned her mother, too, to tell her she was returning to Italy. But, although Mrs Horton asked, she didn't tell her why. That could wait until she got back. She then spent the next twelve hours fretting over whether she was doing the right thing. And, if she was, whether the *marchesa* would agree with her.

The flight proved uneventful, but when she arrived in Pisa she found she had no hope of hiring a car. Instead, she was forced to hire a taxi, and spent the journey worrying that the remaining lira she'd saved from her previous trip would not be enough to cover the fare. She could have asked, of course, before she got into the cab, but she didn't. If the driver had refused to take her, she didn't know what she'd have done.

In the event, paying the man proved to be the least of her problems. Getting him to stay while she spoke to the *marchesa* was another matter, and she was struggling to find the words to make him understand that she would need a ride back to Pisa that evening when she heard the sound of horse's hooves. Glancing apprehensively around, she was relieved to see it was only Ceci who was cantering towards her, her expression mirroring her surprise at the unexpected guest.

'Grace!' she exclaimed, swinging down from the horse's back and bestowing her usual greeting on Grace's cheeks. 'What are you doing here?' She frowned at the unusual sight of a taxi parked on the forecourt of the villa. 'Where's Papà?'

Grace avoided an answer. 'Could you do me a favour, Ceci?' she said instead. 'I'm trying to explain to this man that I'd like him to wait while—while I speak to your great-grandmother.'

'To Nonna?' Ceci frowned. 'Why? What's happened to Papà?'

'Nothing, so far as I know.' Grace had no wish to get involved in a discussion about Matteo. But she was relieved to hear that he obviously wasn't here. 'Please.' She gestured towards the driver. 'Will you tell him I'll want to go back to Pisa tonight?'

Ceci frowned. 'To Pisa?' she said blankly. And then, as if growing impatient with the man's curious stare, she seemed to come to a decision. Grace didn't know what she said to him; it was far too rapid. But the driver tipped a hand to his forehead and got back into his cab.

It wasn't until he drove away that she suspected Ceci hadn't done as she asked. As the cloud of dust the taxi's tyres had churned up subsided, she turned to find the girl handing the reins of her mount to one of the men who had been working in the gardens. Then, tucking her arm through Grace's, Ceci drew her up the steps to the terrace.

'Nonna is resting,' she said, and Grace, who was getting hotter and hotter by the minute, couldn't say she was surprised. Italy in August was a lot different from Italy in June, and the navy trouser suit, which had seemed so cool and comfortable in London, was beginning to cling to her sweating limbs.

'Ceci, what did you tell that man?' she asked, still hoping that the girl might have suggested he go and find a *trattoria* in the village for half an hour or so while she conducted her business. But she was disappointed.

'I told him you'd make other arrangements to get back to Pisa,' declared Ceci unrepentantly. 'You will.' She said this as Grace looked anxious. 'Now, let's sit on the *loggia*. I'm sure you're dying for a long cool drink.'

Grace gave her a tired look. 'Ceci, you know I can't stay here.'

'I know Nonna would be most upset if she knew you doubted her hospitality,' responded Matteo's daughter smoothly. 'Now, you sit here, and I'll go and tell Signora Carlucci that we have a guest for dinner—'

'No—'

But Ceci had already gone, and Grace was left to kick her heels among the exotic overflow from the *marchesa*'s garden. She didn't sit down. She felt as if she'd done nothing but sit down all day. But she did shed her sticky jacket, breathing a little more easily when her bare arms were no longer encased in such formal attire.

She was standing by the windows, staring out at the

lengthening shadows, when a voice said, 'Grace?' in a faintly disbelieving tone, and she turned to find the *marchesa* herself leaning on her cane just inside the door. The old lady stared at her blankly for a few seconds, and then, as if having assured herself that she wasn't hallucinating, she came slowly into the room. 'I thought I heard a car.' She shook her head. 'Where's Matteo?'

This was the second time that someone had suggested that she might know where Matteo was, and this time Grace didn't attempt to avoid an answer. 'I—assume he's still in London,' she said tightly. Then, before she could lose her nerve, she began, 'Marchesa, I hope you'll forgive me for coming here.'

The *marchesa* halted some distance from her, and judging from her expression Grace thought the old lady looked a little confused. As well she might, Grace mused uneasily, aware of her own presumption in thinking the *marchesa* might be willing to take her side against that of her beloved grandson.

'I suppose Ceci was here to greet you,' she said, gesturing towards an arrangement of cane chairs. 'I suggest we sit down. Then you can tell me what you meant by that remark.'

Grace gave an inward groan. 'Look, I probably should explain—'

'Yes, I'm hoping you will.' The *marchesa* lowered herself carefully into one of the chairs. 'Have you ordered tea?'

'I think Ceci—' Grace broke off and, leaving the window, came across to where the old lady was sitting. 'I don't think you understand.'

'I'm sure I don't,' agreed the *marchesa*, tapping the adjoining chair with the head of her cane. 'Sit down, child, do. I'm too old to tip my head back to look at you.'

Grace sighed, but she dropped down into the chair as requested, and sandwiched her damp palms between her knees. 'I'm sorry. I should have waited until tomorrow morning. But I've only got a couple of days, you see.'

The *marchesa* frowned. 'First of all, tell me why you've left Matteo in London.'

'Why *I've*—' Grace pressed a startled hand to her chest. '*I* haven't left Matteo anywhere.'

The *marchesa* frowned. 'But you have seen him?'

'Some time ago, yes.' Grace admitted it reluctantly, feeling her embarrassment burning in her face. 'But that's not—'

'Why you're here?' The old lady looked concerned. 'Forgive me, my dear, but I don't understand. Matteo left for London yesterday, expressly to see you.'

Grace was glad she was sitting down. 'I beg your pardon?' she said, in a voice that sounded little like her own. 'I—think you must have made a mistake.'

'Have I?' The *marchesa*'s frown deepened, and she looked up in some relief when her great-granddaughter came back into the room. 'Ceci,' she said weakly, 'your father did say he was going to see—' She broke off, waving a frail hand in Grace's direction. 'Didn't he?'

'Sì, Nonna.'

Ceci answered in the positive, and Grace saw the old lady's tension subside. 'Thank God!' she declared. 'I was afraid I was getting senile.'

'Not you, Nonna,' Ceci assured her gently, coming to put a reassuring hand on her shoulder. 'I've ordered something long and cool for Grace. And I thought you might like some tea.'

'What would I do without you, my dear?' The *marchesa* patted the girl's hand in response. She turned back to Grace. 'So—you say you did not come here because Matteo invited you. Might I ask when you left England? Was it this morning?'

Grace expelled a breath. 'This morning, yes.' She was still confused and she feared it would take more than Ceci's kindness to reassure her. She hesitated. 'I did speak with—

with Julia a few days ago. She's in London, too, as I'm sure you know. Matteo is most probably with her.'

Which was as it should be, she reminded herself fiercely, suppressing the traitorous excitement she'd felt at the old lady's words. Whatever business Matteo had with her, it was not something to get excited about, and she was glad she had left as she had and avoided a confrontation with him.

Neither the *marchesa* nor her great-granddaughter had made any response to her interpretation of events, but Grace intercepted the look they exchanged with a feeling of unease. She had the feeling that something was going on here that she didn't know about, and she wondered if it had anything to do with the reasons that had brought her to Italy.

The maid's appearance with a tray broke the awkward silence that had fallen between them, and Grace accepted a glass of chilled lemonade with some relief. She was thirsty, and the tension she was feeling was causing the pulse in her head to thump like a hammer. She hoped she wasn't getting a headache. That was all she needed with the prospect of a taxi ride back to Pisa airport ahead of her.

'So, my dear.' Apparently the *marchesa* was still prepared to give her a hearing. 'Perhaps you'd like to tell me what brought you here?' She held up her hand, a diamond ring fit to rival Julia's sparkling on her finger. 'Not that I'm not pleased to see you, of course. But I am—curious.'

Grace put down her glass, using her thumb to wipe the moisture from the corners of her mouth. Then, almost involuntarily, she looked at Ceci, and the *marchesa* nodded in shrewd understanding.

'Go and ask Signora Carlucci to have a room prepared for our guest, my dear,' she said, patting Ceci's hand again, and although Grace made an instinctive gesture of denial the girl was already on her way out of the room. 'Now,' went on her hostess, 'you can speak freely.'

Grace hesitated. 'I don't know where to begin.'

'The beginning is usual,' declared the old lady drily. 'Despite what you said, I apprehend that this *is* about my grandson. Come along. What has he done now?'

Grace's lips twitched. 'You make him sound like a small boy.'

'No. Perhaps a rather gullible older one,' replied the *marchesa* crisply. 'We'll see. Please go on.'

Grace took a breath. 'When—when Matteo came to see me some weeks ago, I inadvertently betrayed a family confidence to him.'

The *marchesa* frowned. 'A family confidence?'

'That's right.' Grace started to pick up her glass again and then thought better of it. 'My—my brother-in-law had just been—well, dismissed from his job.'

'And this was the confidence?'

'Part of it.' Grace forced herself to go on. 'Giles—that's my brother-in-law—I'm afraid he likes gambling—'

'There's no need to go into intimate details, my dear.'

'There is.' Grace shook her head. 'That was why he was fired, you see. Because he—borrowed—some money from his firm's petty cash.'

'Ah.' The old lady took a sip of tea from a bone china cup. 'He was lucky to get away with just being fired. Not all employers are so generous.'

'Well, his employers weren't, you see.' Grace's shoulders sagged. 'They were going to prefer charges. Giles was facing possible prosecution.'

The *marchesa* tilted her head. '*Was* facing? I take it he's not any more?'

'No.' Grace shook her head again.

'And this is because of something Matteo has done?' murmured the old lady astutely. 'But you don't seem pleased about it. Is there something else I should know?'

Grace heaved a sigh. 'Not something I want to talk about,' she said, after a moment. 'I—just don't think Matteo should have interfered. Particularly not when—

when it wasn't anything to do with him,' she finished
lamely.

'I see.' The old lady looked pensive now. 'But, as you
now know, Matteo is not here.'

'It wasn't Matteo I came to see,' said Grace impulsively.
'I wanted—I hoped—you might agree to let me pay the
money back.'

The *marchesa* gave her a bewildered look. 'But this has
nothing to do with me.'

'I know that.' Grace paused. 'But I'd rather not have to
deal with Matteo.'

There was another of those pregnant pauses, and Grace
took the opportunity to finish her lemonade. She didn't
know when she'd get another chance of refreshment.
Whatever the *marchesa* had said earlier, she had the feeling
the explanation she'd given for being here hadn't met with
wholehearted approval, and it was far more likely that she'd
be advised to take the matter up with Matteo himself.
Perhaps when he returned from his honeymoon, she thought
bitterly. She could imagine how humiliating that would be.

A footman appeared just then to turn on the lamps, and
Grace got to her feet.

'I'm sure you'd like me to leave now,' she said, hooking
the strap of her tote bag over her shoulder. 'If I could just
use your phone—'

'What are you talking about, child?' The *marchesa*
seemed to thrust off whatever worry had caused a groove
to appear between her brows and tapped the floor with her
cane. 'I thought I'd made myself very plain. Naturally,
you'll spend the night at the villa. I won't hear of you
travelling back to your hotel tonight. If you'll give me the
details, I'll have Aldo go and collect the rest of your belongings—'

Grace moved a little awkwardly. 'I—didn't check in to
a hotel, Marchesa.'

'All the better, then.' The *marchesa* studied her for a
moment. 'So where is your suitcase?'

'I didn't bring a suitcase,' admitted Grace ruefully. 'Just—just a change of underwear. That sort of thing.'

'You young people,' said the *marchesa* wryly, but she didn't sound as if she was surprised. 'Very well. Ceci will lend you anything else you need. I'm sure she's got something in her wardrobe that you can wear this evening. We dine at nine, as you know.'

'But, Marchesa—'

'We'll talk later,' the old lady said firmly, and there was no gainsaying her. 'Ring the bell, will you? I'm sure Signora Carlucci will have your room ready by now.'

Grace had a disturbing feeling of *déjà vu* as the maid escorted her to her room. Once again, she was to be accommodated in the east wing, and she felt a treacherous sense of pleasure when she was shown into the apartments she had occupied before. There should have been bitterness, and the memory of betrayal, but instead there was warmth and familiarity. She hadn't realised how much she'd wanted to come back here, and she wondered if that was why she hadn't tried harder to get in touch with the *marchesa* some other way.

She had showered and changed her underwear and was sitting at the dressing table drying her hair when she heard the now familiar knock at her door. But it couldn't be Matteo, she assured herself. He was still in London. So she wrapped the folds of a bathrobe about her, and called, 'Come in.'

It was Ceci. The younger girl was carrying a sheaf of garments draped over her arm, and she came into the suite of rooms with a diffident smile. 'Nonna said you needed something to wear for dinner,' she explained, indicating the clothes. 'I don't know if anything here is suitable. I'm afraid nothing of mine would do.'

Grace got to her feet. 'Really, you shouldn't have bothered…'

'What? And have Nonna accuse me of letting her down?'

Ceci grimaced. 'No, honestly, I'd have been happy to help you out, but I'm afraid I'm not as tall or as—as—'

'Broad?'

'—shapely,' Ceci said firmly, 'as you.'

Grace came towards her with a wry smile, touching the jewel-toned fabric of a skirt with an admiring finger. 'But where did you get these from?'

'They were my grandmother's,' admitted Ceci ruefully, and Grace withdrew her hand in alarm.

'Your grandmother's clothes!' She caught her breath. 'Well, it's very kind of you, of course, but—'

'They're in excellent condition,' protested Ceci at once, misunderstanding her. 'They've been kept aired, and they're pressed regularly—'

'That's not the point—'

'Nonna's always saying she's going to send them to a church benefit or something. I suppose they might be worth something to a collector.'

'Ceci…' Grace sighed. 'The clothes are beautiful! And I'm flattered that you should offer them to me. But—' she shook her head '—I couldn't wear your grandmother's clothes. It wouldn't be right.'

'I don't think Papà would agree.'

Grace's face filled with colour. 'Ceci—'

'I mean it,' said Ceci, laying the garments almost reverently on the bed. 'It's not as if he remembers his mother wearing them. And Nonna said it was fitting that you and she should be of a similar size.'

Grace didn't know what to say. She didn't want to offend the girl, but she wondered what the *marchesa* was doing, filling Ceci's head with such nonsense. If this was another power-play against Julia, then she should be ashamed of herself. The Englishwoman might not have been her choice for a granddaughter-in-law, but with the baby Julia was carrying all bets were off.

'Look,' Grace said now, 'I really am thrilled that you

and your great-grandmother should offer me the chance to wear one of these gowns, but—'

'You don't like them?'

'Of course I like them.' Grace didn't see how anyone couldn't like such delicate things. 'But—well, it's not my place, don't you see? It's—it's Julia you should be offering them to. Not me.'

Ceci squared her shoulders. 'Julia's gone away,' she said, pushing her hands into the pockets of her riding breeches. 'Nonna said I wasn't to say anything, that it wasn't up to me, but I think you ought to know.'

Grace stared at her warily. Of course Julia had gone away. She knew that. She'd never forget that awful scene in Julia's suite at the Dorchester. But why would the *marchesa* warn Ceci against discussing it when she knew Grace had seen Julia in London?

'I don't think that matters,' she said now, recognising the anxiety in Ceci's face. The girl was regretting what she'd said. She could tell. 'Look, I won't say anything about this conversation. Let's forget it ever happened, okay?'

Ceci moved her shoulders in a gesture that could have meant anything, but Grace started when the girl pulled a hand out of her pocket to touch the other woman's hair. 'You're so lucky,' she said, 'having hair like this. Mine takes forever to grow.' She combed a hand through her own ruffled curls. 'I've always wanted to be a blonde.'

'But your hair's beautiful,' protested Grace, Ceci's resemblance to Matteo never more evident than at that moment. 'Believe me, blondes do not have more fun!'

Ceci dimpled. 'Don't you think so?'

'No. Definitely not,' Grace assured her. 'But I'm sure you know that for yourself. You can't have got through your first year of college without collecting your fair share of admirers.'

'Well...' Ceci was modest. 'There have been one or two...'

'Including the young man your father spoke about?' suggested Grace, feeling a bittersweet pang at the memory of her first evening at the villa, and the girl chuckled.

'Domenico,' she said, nodding. 'He's all right, I suppose. But too serious, if you know what I mean?'

'Is there such a thing?' Grace was ironic, and then, realising Ceci was studying her with a replica of her father's intensity, she looped the long coil of hair over one shoulder. 'And now, if you'll excuse me, I must finish drying this...'

'And you will wear one of Nonna Elena's gowns, won't you?' Ceci persisted, heading towards the door, proving that she hadn't been diverted from her original task. She smiled into Grace's frustrated face. 'Nonna will not be pleased if you disappoint her.'

Grace could believe that. Between them, Matteo and his grandmother had more than their fair share of arrogance, and she could quite see that if she turned up for dinner wearing the same clothes she had travelled in the old lady would be put out, to say the least. Particularly after she had gone to the trouble of providing her with an alternative.

And what an alternative. After Ceci had gone, Grace approached the pile of clothes she had left on the bed with reluctant interest. The girl had evidently not been able to decide what to choose and, as well as the skirt Grace had admired earlier, there was a flowing georgette trouser suit, two silk cocktail dresses, and an elaborate embroidered tunic. To wear with the skirt, Grace guessed, realising the two items would look well together.

But the garment which caught her attention was an ankle-length gown of gossamer-thin chiffon. Its style was simple enough: delicate cap sleeves and a modestly rounded neckline curved gently into the waist, before dropping, tube-like, to the hem. There was an equally delicate chemise to wear underneath, and the colour, a seadrift blend of grey and green, was more subtle than the others.

Grace knew, as soon as she put it on, that she would wear it. Despite her doubts, despite her misgivings, the *marchesa* evidently knew her better than she knew herself,

and the old lady must have guessed she would not be able
to resist such a lovely thing. It fitted her so perfectly, it
could have been made for her, outlining the generous
curves of her body with an elegance at once flattering and
statuesque.

She thought about leaving her hair loose, but somehow
that didn't go with what she was wearing. A chignon would
have been more dignified, but she doubted her hair, soft
and silky from its washing, would allow itself to be con-
fined that way. She compromised by threading a thin silk
scarf she found among the clothes into a loose braid, and
was pleasantly surprised when she saw herself. Both the
gown and the hairstyle had a vaguely medieval look.

Just right for a villa whose origins were lost in the mists
of time, she thought, glad that she had been wearing sandals
and not shoes when she caught the plane. She doubted
Ceci's grandmother's shoes would have fitted her feet.

She felt terribly self-conscious, nonetheless, when she
left her rooms. Despite the underslip, she had never worn
such a revealing dress before. Yet revealing wasn't the right
word, she acknowledged. In many ways, it was excessively
demure. No, if she was honest, she would admit that the
gown displayed the fact that it had been designed and sewn
by a master craftsman. It was chic and sexy, without looking obvious.

The *loggia*, where they had gathered for pre-dinner
drinks the last time she was here, was shadowy in lamp-
light. For a moment she thought the place was deserted,
and she was just wondering whether she'd made a mistake
in thinking they were meeting here when a shadow, deeper
than the rest, moved unexpectedly into the light.

'Hello, *cara*,' said Matteo softly, and her skin prickled
as if he had stroked it. 'Dare I say, you have never looked
lovelier than you do this evening? Thank God you had the
presence of mind to tell your mother where you were
going.'

CHAPTER FOURTEEN

GRACE stared at him in dismay. 'What are you doing here?'

Matteo lifted his shoulders, his olive skin dark beneath the thin silk of his white shirt. 'I live here,' he said, flattening his hands in the back pockets of his black trousers. 'As you well know.'

'That's not what I meant.' Grace twisted her hands together nervously, and then, realising how her action might look to him, she thrust them behind her back. 'You're supposed to be in London with—with Julia.'

'I was supposed to be in London with you,' Matteo corrected her flatly. 'I had no idea that you might come here.'

'Didn't you?'

He frowned. 'No.'

Grace squared her shoulders. 'Not even to correct your assumption that I needed some—compensation?'

'Compensation? What are you talking about?'

'Don't pretend you don't know.' Grace refused to be swayed by his apparent bewilderment. 'I'm sure you knew Julia would tell me all about it. How you felt obliged to get Giles out of his difficulties as a way of salving your conscience for the way you'd treated me!'

'You're crazy!' Matteo's eyes darkened. 'You can't believe I helped your brother-in-law for some selfish reason of my own!'

Grace shrugged. 'Well, I don't see how you can deny it. If you hadn't discussed it with Julia, she'd have known nothing about it.'

Matteo swore then. 'You are so quick to judge me, aren't you, Grace?' he exclaimed, his accent becoming evident as his anger got the better of him. 'I do not know what Julia has told you, but I did not discuss your brother-in-law with her. I have not seen her since she left here a week ago. Nor do I intend to. Our association—such as it was—is at an end.'

Grace gasped. 'But what about the baby?'

'There was no baby,' said Matteo grimly. 'That was just another of her lies.'

'No!'

'Oh, yes.' His lips twisted. 'So you see, I, too, have much to be bitter about. But I do not blame you because I was too blind to see the truth for myself.'

Grace couldn't believe it. 'But she said—'

'Yes?' Matteo regarded her intently. 'What did she say? Apart from these lies she must have hoped you'd bring to me?'

'She said—she let me think that—that you two were still together. She had a watch; a *ring*.' Grace shook her head. 'She couldn't have afforded to buy them for herself.'

'No.' Matteo's nostrils flared. 'No, of course she couldn't.'

'You mean—you did buy them—?'

'No, I did not.' Matteo was impatient. 'Had it been left to me—' He broke off abruptly, and then continued, 'But it was not. Not entirely, anyway. My grandmother had already promised—' He halted again, his frustration evident. 'Ah, but you do not wish to hear this. Whatever I say, whatever I do, you will always believe the worst.'

'No…' Grace brought her hands to her lips and took an involuntary step towards him. 'No, I won't,' she promised huskily. 'Please, Matteo, I want to know how you found out.'

His eyes softened, almost against his will, it seemed. 'And I am fool enough to be persuaded by your plea,' he said harshly. 'You see what you have done to me?'

'I'm sorry.' She was contrite. 'Julia told me—oh, she made me feel like such an idiot. When you came to the apartment that day, I really believed you meant what you said.'

'I did.' Matteo's voice had thickened. 'But I am forgetting myself.' He gestured towards the table. 'There's wine—and *biscotti*. And Signora Carlucci has prepared a special dinner...' He paused. 'For two.'

'For two?' Grace's lips parted. 'But what about Ceci—and your grandmother?'

'You will find my grandmother can be very sympathetic when it pleases her to be so,' replied Matteo, filling two glasses with a ruby-red vintage. He handed one to her, his fingers brushing hers in an involuntary caress. 'She knew we needed to talk, and she hopes that we may be able to solve our differences.' He raised his glass to his lips and looked at her over the rim. 'Can we?'

Grace quivered inside. 'I suppose that depends what those differences are,' she said, a little nervously. 'Tell me about Julia.'

'Ah, yes.' Matteo's sigh was heavy. 'I suppose it must be now and not later.' He paused. 'First of all, I have to say that Julia never, at any time, believed she was pregnant.'

Grace's eyes went wide. 'No!'

'Oh, yes.' Matteo's gaze was steady. 'I do not know what she told you about that weekend we spent in Rome, but as far as I was concerned there should have been no question of—of—well, of a mistake.' He scowled. '*Dio*, this is so awful! How do you tell the woman you love that when you had sex with her friend you used protection?' He groaned. 'But, of course, there was always the chance—'

'Wait!' Grace stopped him there, putting her glass down on the table as she did so, afraid that her shaking fingers might spill wine on her borrowed gown. 'What—what did you say?'

Matteo's scowl deepened. 'Must I repeat it?' He took a breath. 'That I used protection, of course,' he muttered, a faint flush deepening his tan. 'You asked me to tell you what happened—'

'And I want to know,' Grace assured him urgently. 'But you said something else, something before that. Don't you remember?'

Matteo's brows descended. 'Perhaps you should remind me,' he said thickly, and she suspected then that he knew exactly what she was talking about.

'You said—you said it was hard to tell the woman you love,' she confessed, gazing at him, and his mouth curved with sensual satisfaction.

'So it is,' he murmured, causing an anticipatory shiver to feather her spine. 'And hearing that I love you can't be news to you, *cara*. I said as much that afternoon at your apartment.'

Grace caught her breath. 'But I thought—'

'Yes? What did you think?'

Grace trembled. 'That you were feeling guilty about what had happened between us; that you regretted getting involved…'

'Oh, *cara*, if you only knew.' He put down his glass and stood for a few moments staring down at the wine that still shimmered in it. 'I remember clearly how I felt that afternoon, and my regrets had nothing to do with you.'

Grace hesitated. 'I suppose believing you were being forced to get married again must have been—frustrating.'

'Frustrating?' Matteo looked at her now. '*Cara*, frustration was not my strongest emotion, believe me.'

She did believe him. Unfortunately, she believed him only too well. Whatever feelings he professed to have for her, she must never forget that marriage was not part of his vocabulary.

'Do you want me to go on?' he asked now, and she became aware that he was watching her with disturbingly sensual eyes. 'Or do you want to talk about us?'

'Yes…' Grace realised how her word could be misconstrued, and hurriedly amended it. 'Please—go on.'

Matteo didn't speak for a few moments, and when he did it was not what she expected. 'So you are going to make me wait for you to say the words I long to hear?' he questioned softly. 'Cruel, Grace. Very cruel.'

Her face flamed. 'I had a good teacher,' she said, forcing herself not to give in. 'Please, Matteo: you promised.'

'Very well.' He swayed back on his heels, but she could tell he was disappointed in her answer. 'Where was I? Ah, yes, that fateful weekend in Rome. That must have been when Julia had the idea of using a child to effect a marriage between us.'

Grace shook her head. 'But she wasn't pregnant!'

'No. But she'd obviously intended to be. That part was true enough.'

'I don't understand.'

'Well, her story is that she was not to know that I'd lose interest in her once I'd had my wicked way. The truth is slightly less theatrical. In fact, I never was particularly attracted to her.'

'Then why did you phone her less than twenty-four hours after you'd met?' asked Grace, feeling obliged to defend her friend, and Matteo gave her an old-fashioned look.

'She told you that, I suppose.' His lips twisted. 'And did she also say that she'd made a point of leaving her purse in my car when I was fool enough to drive her and her friend back to where they were staying?'

'No.'

Grace looked chastened, and Matteo took another weary breath before continuing, 'I did go out with her. I'm not denying that. For a few weeks, we saw one another on a fairly regular basis. But it wasn't until I had to go to Rome on business and she asked if she could come along that our relationship became a sexual one. The rest, as they say, is history.'

Grace pressed her palms together. 'So—when she told you she was expecting your baby, you had no reason to doubt her?'

'Oh, I had plenty of reasons for doubting her,' retorted Matteo bitterly. 'Only at that time I was too shocked to think clearly. I believe my grandmother told you how my first wife died?' And at her gesture of assent he went on, 'Then perhaps you'll understand how I was feeling. I was so—gutted—that I'd apparently broken the promise I'd made to myself when Luisa died that I didn't immediately question the validity of Julia's claim.' He groaned. 'My first thought was, Grace will never forgive me for this, and you'd have been right. Dear God, I never would have forgiven myself.'

Grace had to steel herself then to stay where she was. The urge to go to him, to comfort him, to tell him that she'd forgive him anything when he looked at her as he was doing now, was paramount, but somehow she controlled it.

'That was what I meant when I said frustration didn't cover it,' he declared harshly. 'All I could see was that our lives were being shattered by a woman who cared nothing for me; whose only real desire was to have an easy life.'

'I think you underestimate yourself,' murmured Grace wryly, but Matteo only shook his head. 'Besides, she must have known that sooner or later you'd find out.'

'Not necessarily.' Matteo was grim. 'In Julia's world, men are just sexual animals; a collection of uncontrollable hormones, without any care for what's right or wrong. Press the right buttons and they'll perform to order.'

'You mean—'

'I mean, I'm sure she realised that eventually I would find out the truth. But by then, I suppose, she hoped to be pregnant. We'd be married by then and, as she knew I was a Catholic, a divorce would be out of the question.'

Grace was appalled. 'I had no idea.'

'No.' Matteo nodded. 'Although I should have had some suspicion. It is, after all, the oldest trick in the book. The baby gambit! And I fell for it.'

'Oh, Matteo…'

'My only excuse, as I said before, was the guilt I still feel for what happened to Luisa.' He made a defeated gesture. 'Julia had found out about that, of course, and she banked on the fact that, having lost one wife in childbirth, I'd do nothing to risk losing another.' He paused. 'And then there was you.'

'Me?'

Grace stared at him, and he nodded. 'Of course. You validated what Julia said. I thought, If Grace believes it to be true, it must be true.'

'Oh, God!'

'That still doesn't excuse my stupidity. But after you'd left I was in no mood to listen to anyone's advice. Particularly not that of my grandmother. I knew she'd never liked Julia. So anything she said was bound to be biased.'

'So what happened?'

'What happened?' Matteo rubbed his temple with the thumb and forefinger of one hand. 'Well, as I recall it, Julia decided to go back to Portofalco, perhaps hoping that I would follow her, but I spent the next couple of weeks summoning up the courage to come and see you.'

'But you talked to Julia?'

'Oh, yes. And to my grandmother. She urged me to insist that Julia be examined by our own doctor, but after speaking to you I didn't think there was any point in that. It was obvious that you accepted her story completely, and I wasn't to know she'd duped you just as successfully as she'd duped me.'

'So, how...?'

'My grandmother did something very simple and very apposite,' said Matteo ruefully. 'I was away in Genoa, having meetings with our shipping agents, and Nonna went and saw Julia herself. As far as I can gather, she offered her a considerable sum of money if Julia would agree to come back to Valle di Falco and have a physical examination, with the proviso that if she refused Nonna would ensure that a significant period of time elapsed before a wedding could take place.'

Grace caught her breath. 'And Julia agreed?'

'What else could she do? And no doubt that was when she heard what I had done about Giles. I do know Nonna and I discussed it. And Julia was not above using things and people to her own ends, as we know.'

Grace couldn't hide her anguish. 'How could she?'

Matteo shrugged. 'It's not something we need care about now. I wanted to make life easier for you. There was so little I could do in the circumstances. You've no conception of how hard it was leaving you that day.'

Grace thought she had a fair idea, but that could wait till later. 'And, of course, with the examination, Julia was found out?'

'Of course.' Matteo sighed. 'And who knows? Maybe that was her plan all along. She never loved me; that I do know. So here was a way for her to become exceedingly wealthy without the penalty of marrying me.'

Some penalty, thought Grace, but she didn't say anything. She was still reeling from the knowledge that she had almost caused Julia's original plan to succeed.

'She left here almost immediately afterwards,' Matteo went on. 'But I had no idea that she might try to see you. Yet, there again, why not? She'd already done her best to destroy any chance of a relationship between us, and it must have pleased her immensely to taunt you with her apparent success.'

Grace was shaking her head. 'I don't know what to say.'

'That you don't hate me would be a good start,' said Matteo huskily, and she gazed at him with bewildered eyes.

'Hate you?'

'For being such a fool; for taking so long to admit to myself, as well as to you, that I love you.' His eyes caressed her. 'Can you forgive me?'

Grace spread her hands. 'There's nothing to forgive.'

'I disagree.' Matteo captured her hands, pulling her towards him as he drew her hands down to her sides. 'I was afraid, you see. Afraid of my feelings; afraid that you might turn me down.' He searched her face. 'You won't, will you? I need you so much.'

Grace could only stare helplessly at him. 'Is this why you came to England?'

'Why else?' Matteo's breath was warm against her cheek. 'I should have got to your apartment yesterday evening, but my flight was delayed—'

'The air traffic controllers' strike.'

'The strike. That's right.' Matteo nodded. 'It was after midnight by the time I reached the city so I checked into a hotel—'

'Not—not the Dorchester?' she breathed, still barely able to believe what was happening to her, and Matteo frowned.

'No. The Savoy,' he said uncomprehendingly. 'Does it matter?'

'No.' Grace shook her head, content that her doubts about the man who had answered Julia's phone had not been misplaced. 'But you spoke to my mother?'

'I rang her this morning when I discovered you were neither at work nor at your apartment. She seemed—unsurprised that I was looking for you.'

Grace smiled. 'My mother is an optimist.'

'What is that supposed to mean?'

'It doesn't matter.' Grace explored his face with a hunger she'd hardly dared to acknowledge until now. 'You came back. That's what matters.'

'Does it?' Matteo released her hands to cup her face between his spread fingers. 'Oh, *cara*, have you any idea of how I felt that morning when Julia said the words that almost ruined my life?'

'I think I have a fair idea,' she responded, a little breathily. 'Even though I thought your behaviour was—was totally reprehensible.'

Matteo groaned, his thumbs probing the faint lines beneath her eyes. 'That was your fault,' he murmured, brushing her mouth with his in a tantalising little caress. 'I wasn't prepared for the fact that meeting Julia had just been fate's way of bringing us together.' He kissed her again, more deeply. 'I knew, from the minute you opened the door of Julia's apartment, and looked at me in that supercilious way you have, that you and I had unfinished business.'

Grace protested. 'I don't have a supercilious look,' she cried, and Matteo's hands slid possessively to the back of her scalp.

'Yes, you do. And I love it,' he assured her softly. 'Just as I love every single thing about you. I want you. I want you so much, *cara*. I want to kiss you, and hold you, and make love with you—' He broke off abruptly, resting his forehead against hers as he fought for restraint. 'But,' he went on, 'you haven't eaten, and Signora Carlucci is expecting us to do justice to her most excellent dinner—'

'I'm not hungry,' said Grace at once, and Matteo expelled an unsteady breath.

'I am,' he told her honestly. 'But only for you.'

'So...' She trembled.

'So, come with me,' he said, his voice rough with passion, and she took the hand he held out to her without hesitation.

She was hardly aware of where he was taking her, only that this was not the way to her apartments. But she would have followed him to the ends of the earth, she thought, quivering a little at how vulnerable that made her.

When they finally arrived at their destination, she knew that these were Matteo's rooms. Heavy wooden doors opened into a lamplit sitting room that was essentially masculine in design, with deep armchairs upholstered in glove-soft leather and thick velvet drapes at the long windows. The curtains in the living room weren't drawn, and through the windows she could see the lights twinkling across the valley.

Unlike her apartments, which had a door to divide the rooms, here an archway revealed the adjoining apartment where a huge four-poster bed was set squarely on a dais. The curtains were drawn across the windows in the bedroom, creating an intensely intimate atmosphere that she could not ignore.

Matteo closed the outer door and came to stand beside her as she lingered by the archway. 'Don't blame me,' he said softly, looking at the bed. 'It's a family heirloom.'

Grace took a breath and then, turning towards him, put her hands up to his face. 'Is it comfortable?' she asked provocatively, and Matteo pulled her possessively into her arms.

'Do you want to find out?' he asked, looking deeply into her eyes, and she felt her heart turn over with love for him.

'Please,' she breathed, her hands dropping to the open neck of his shirt and lingering against his warm skin. 'But I think I'd better take your mother's gown off first.'

'Let me,' he said, his hands moving surely to the buttons at the back of her neck. Then, turning her round, he bent his mouth to the soft flesh he'd exposed. 'I hoped you'd choose this one,' he added, his fingers causing a gathering swell of sensation to ripple down her spine. 'Nonna had a picture of my mother wearing it when she was about your age, and it was always my favourite.'

Grace swung round as he peeled the outer layer of the dress away. 'You chose it?' she exclaimed. 'But Ceci said—'

'What I told her to say,' Matteo informed her, with gentle arrogance. 'Do you mind?'

Grace glanced down at her breasts, her nipples taut against the fine silk of the undergarment. 'Is there any point?' she asked helplessly, and he lifted his hands to cover the rebellious peaks.

'Not really,' he conceded, his palms driving her mad with the desire to feel them against her naked flesh.

And, as if he knew exactly how she was feeling, he released the shoulder fastenings then so that the slip pooled about her feet. Her bra—a rather plain eyelet cotton—followed it, and she was left wearing only cotton bikini briefs.

Matteo gazed at her with obvious hunger for a moment, and then his hands went to the buttons of his own shirt. 'Help me,' he said as her eyes followed his hands down to where his erection swelled the front of his black trousers, and, kicking off her sandals, Grace obeyed.

But when she would have knelt to ease the trousers off his legs Matteo could stand it no longer. 'Don't,' he groaned, flinging off his shirt and balancing on each leg in turn to free himself from the constriction of his trousers. Then, when he had rid himself of his silk boxers as well, he pulled her against him.

It was the first time she had felt his naked body against hers and the sensation was incredible. He was so hot, his skin coarser than hers, except between his legs where it was as silky soft as it had been in her dream.

'Do you know how much I've longed for this moment?' he said, his voice muffled against the curve of her neck. 'When I thought I'd lost you, I used to torment myself with images of you with some other man.'

'I dreamed about you,' confessed Grace, lifting her shoulder to his seeking lips. She spread her palms against his chest. 'But it wasn't as good as this.'

'Nothing's ever been as good as this,' muttered Matteo, pulling her even closer. His manhood thrust urgently against her stomach. 'I've never wanted any other woman as I've wanted you.'

Her sigh whispered against his throat, her knees sagging as he caressed her breasts. Every sensation he was inspiring seemed to be centred on her stomach and between her legs, tiny darts of excitement that tightened her muscles and moistened her skin.

His hands moved to grip her upper arms, sliding up and down, up and down, as his mouth finally sought her parted lips. His tongue thrust into her mouth, filling her with its

heat and maleness, a hot wet possession that brought her
arching helplessly towards him.

He stroked her back now, his fingers finding all the sensitive pulses of her spine, before his thumbs hooked the
waistband of her briefs. With his mouth devouring hers,
she could only give a little moan of pleasure as he peeled
the briefs away, and then the power of his arousal nudged
the silvery crest that hid her sex.

It was too much; she had to clutch his neck to prevent
herself from falling, and, containing his own impatience,
Matteo drew her across to the bed. Grace wasn't sure if she
was going to make it, but he swung her up into his arms,
and, climbing onto the dais, he lowered her gently onto the
soft quilt.

He knelt beside her then, taking the time to loosen her
hair from its braid and spread her hair on the pillows as
he'd once promised he would. The silk scarf he fanned
across her breasts, before suckling her through its gauzy
sheath, and Grace found there was something incredibly
erotic in his actions, her breasts twice as sensitised when
he drew the gauze away.

He traced the line of her stomach down to her navel,
following his fingers with his tongue, licking away the
heated moisture that filmed her skin. He parted her legs,
finding the delicate petals that opened to his fingers, stroking the cleft that pulsated between her legs.

But when Grace would have stroked his erection he
gripped her hand around him in instant denial. 'No, *cara*,'
he said, 'my control is far too thin. Let me please you first;
let me play with your body a little longer; it responds so
sweetly.' He bent her leg and insinuated a tantalising kiss
behind her knee. 'You see,' he said, when she jerked automatically against him. 'I want to taste every inch of you
tonight.'

'But, Matteo...'

Grace sighed, levering herself up on her elbows, and with
a lithe shift he stretched his length beside her. 'What,

cara?' he asked huskily, his thumb teasing the edge of her desire, and when she looked down and groaned he pushed his thumb into her aching flesh.

It was all that was needed. Her body bucked beneath his hands, and her low moan of surrender seemed to sear his need. 'Now, *cara*,' he said, moving to kneel between her legs as the shock waves of emotions reached a climax. And, sliding his hands beneath her rounded bottom, he lifted her to meet his thrusting shaft.

Grace hadn't believed it could get any better, but it did. When Matteo impaled her, the pleasure she was feeling rose in counterpoint to his need. For a few brief moments they rode together to the rim of the volcano, then Matteo's explosive climax tore the barriers away.

It was like falling through space. Her mind ceased to react, and her senses took over. Her body throbbed in the aftermath of an almost spiritual fulfilment, the physical tremors she was feeling echoing deep inside her soul.

For the first time she realised the difference between having sex and making love. Matteo had just made love with her, and the weight of his body crushing hers into the mattress was a privilege and not an invasion.

She was smoothing the damp hair at the nape of his neck when Matteo stirred and rolled immediately onto his side, facing her. 'I'm sorry,' he said huskily. 'I'm afraid I haven't been very sensible, have I?'

'Sensible?' Grace frowned. 'I don't understand.'

'I didn't use any protection,' replied Matteo roughly, using both hands to comb back his hair. He propped himself up on one elbow, stifling a profanity as he did so. 'I'll make sure it doesn't happen next time.'

Grace took a breath. 'So there is going to be a next time, then?' she murmured carefully, and his eyes darkened with unmistakable impatience.

'What are you saying?' he demanded. 'I want you to marry me. My God, you didn't think I meant anything else?'

Grace quivered. 'I didn't know, did I?' she protested, her excitement scarcely held in check now. 'You did say you had no intention of getting married again.'

'A foolish boast,' he said, his fingers brushing her lips. 'Particularly as I already couldn't bear to leave you alone.'

Grace frowned again. 'Then why does it matter whether you used any protection or not? If I'm to be your wife...'

'Which is why it matters so much,' replied Matteo, his voice thickening with emotion. 'I will not risk losing you, *cara*, however much I might wish to see my child swelling your stomach.'

Grace caught her breath. 'But I'm not Luisa, Matteo!'

'No.' He conceded the point with a lingering kiss on the silky mound of her breast. 'No, you're not. But, God forgive me, you mean more to me than Luisa ever did, and I don't think I could survive losing you.'

'You're not going to lose me.' Grace turned and cupped his face in her hand. 'Matteo, I'm probably nothing like Luisa—physically, I mean.' She grimaced. 'My hips are broad. I'm sure I'd have no trouble having a child.'

'I will not risk it.' Matteo's voice was flat. 'If you love me, you'll understand how I feel. If not—'

'If not—what?'

'Well, I won't let you go,' he declared grimly. 'I'll just have to try and persuade you, that's all.'

Grace shook her head. 'You know I love you. That I want to marry you whatever you decide.'

'And you won't reproach me for denying you your right to be a mother?'

Grace shook her head. 'If it's a choice between you and a baby...' she smiled wistfully '...I guess there's no competition.'

EPILOGUE

One Year and Nine Months Later...

THE sound of children's laughter echoed through the open doors of the *loggia*. Three-year-old Hannah was chasing her sister and her five-year-old cousin around the gardens, and the *marchesa* turned to give her granddaughter-in-law a rueful smile.

'It's so good to have children at the villa again,' she said, reassuring Grace that her nieces' high spirits weren't proving too much of a burden. And it was good to be able to invite her sisters and their families for a holiday. They had so much room at the villa that no one needed to step on anyone else's toes.

'I'll be sorry to see them go,' added the *marchesa*, patting Grace's arm with an affectionate hand. 'But I'm lucky that you and Matteo are prepared to put up with an old woman like me. If Matteo had married someone else, I might not have had the choice.'

Grace reached across to squeeze the *marchesa*'s fingers. 'This is your home,' she said. 'It always has been. Even when Matteo was married to Luisa.'

'Ah, yes.' The *marchesa* nodded. 'But Matteo married Luisa to please me. When he chose to marry you, it was a different matter altogether.'

Grace's cheeks turned pink. 'Did you mind?'

'Of course not.' The old lady was impatient that she should even doubt it. 'I love my grandson, Grace, and I know he's never been so happy in his life. I have you to thank for that, and that alone would have earned you my undying gratitude. But the bonus of it is that I've come to love you, too.'

Grace didn't know what to say. 'I'm glad,' seemed inadequate, but it evidently pleased her companion.

'And you and Cecilia have become such friends,' the *marchesa* continued, gazing at her contentedly. 'I know when she and Domenico are married she'll be coming to you for all those important words of motherly advice.'

Grace grimaced. 'I don't know if I'm qualified for that,' she murmured, although she was delighted that Ceci and Domenico were engaged at last. He was such a nice young man, and he and Matteo had hit it off together. When he'd finished his degree, he was coming to work at the winery, and Matteo was going to teach him about growing grapes.

'Well, I don't know anyone better,' declared the old lady firmly, tapping her cane as she always did to make her point. 'When did you say your mother and the others were getting back from Florence? They must be here for the party. They must watch when Beniamino blows out the candle on his cake.'

Grace stretched lazily on the lounger. 'I expect they'll be here in plenty of time,' she assured the *marchesa*, with an indulgent smile. 'Oh, you know, I feel as if I've eaten too much pasta. I'll have to watch my weight or I'll be as fat as butter!'

'I don't think that's very likely,' remarked the old lady drily, viewing her granddaughter-in-law's lissome figure with an indulgent eye. She paused. 'Have you told Matteo that you're expecting another baby yet? Be prepared for him to have mixed feelings. He nearly went out of his mind with worry when Beniamino was born.'

Grace sat up rather abruptly. 'How did you know?' she asked, running a protective hand over her flat stomach, and the *marchesa* sighed.

'Women know these things, my dear,' she said. 'Well, old women, anyway. But tell him, Grace. Don't wait for him to find out for himself.'

Grace shook her head. It was true, when Matteo had learned that she had conceived that first night they had been together he had cursed his own incompetence. But gradually, over the weeks and months after their wedding, as Grace had grown even more beautiful in pregnancy, he had managed to hide his fears. And when their son was born it had happened so quickly, he hadn't had time to do anything but be there for her, sponging her forehead during the painful contractions, holding her hand as the baby thrust its way into the world.

Grace had soon realised that she was a natural mother. She'd fed Beniamino herself until he was six months old, and Matteo had shared every experience with her. There had been something so intensely intimate in Matteo watching his son suckling from her breast, and he'd confessed to feeling jealous until she'd assured him he had nothing to fear.

But another baby…

She suspected the *marchesa* was right—that Matteo would not be pleased that she was pregnant again. Even though having Beniamino had been comparatively easy, he still insisted that once was enough. But accidents happened, even in the best of circles, and Grace was sure her husband was unaware of what he'd done. Which meant she would have to tell him that his methods weren't always foolproof, after all.

Matteo appeared at that moment, carrying their baby son, giving a defensive smile when Grace pulled a face at him. 'He was awake,' he insisted. 'And it is his birthday, when all's said and done. Why shouldn't he enjoy his party?' He listened to the sound of the children for a moment. 'Everyone else seemed to be doing so.'

Grace held out her arms and Matteo handed the baby to her as the *marchesa* got to her feet. 'I think I'll take a rest, after all,' she said, giving Grace a speaking look. 'Let me know when the others get back.'

'We will,' said Matteo, subsiding into the chair she'd

vacated. He tipped his head in Grace's direction as she fussed with Beniamino, who was clutching the gold necklace she was wearing. 'I get the feeling Nonna's departure was pre-arranged.'

Grace caught her breath. 'Why should you think that?' she exclaimed, her hand sliding over the baby's silky head. 'No, you're not getting down,' she told the little boy, who was wriggling impatiently. 'You have to keep clean today. It's your birthday.'

'Let him get down,' Matteo advised her lazily. 'Antonia can change him if he gets into a mess.' Antonia was Beniamino's nanny, and Grace conceded that the girl would be only too happy to take charge of him. It was her happy choice that she spent so much time looking after him herself.

'All right.'

She set Beniamino on his feet, and he toddled away across the tiled floor. Antonia appeared at once, ever vigilant, from her position at the end of the *loggia*, and Grace relaxed as the nanny took the baby's hand.

'Now.' Matteo leant towards her with warm indulgence. 'Are you going to tell me why my grandmother decided we needed to be alone?' His eyes searched her face. 'It couldn't have anything to do with that box I found in the waste bin in our bathroom, could it?'

Grace's face flamed. 'Since when do you go looking in waste bins?'

'Since I dropped a blade from my razor and it fell into the bin,' replied her husband, without hesitation. 'It was a pregnancy testing kit, I believe. Which is why you've been avoiding being alone with me, isn't it?'

Grace gasped. 'I haven't been avoiding being alone with you,' she protested. 'We sleep together—alone—every night.'

Matteo's brows arched. 'But you have been significantly non-communicative. You've pretended to be asleep every night when I've come to bed.'

'Only because you've been staying up late with Giles and David.'

'Late?' Matteo pulled a wry face. 'Half-past ten is not late, *cara*, and you know it. And I'd rather be with you, as you're aware.'

Grace expelled a breath. 'All right. All right. I'm pregnant.' She hunched her shoulders. 'I was afraid to tell you, that's all. I know you didn't want another baby. I—I didn't arrange it to happen, if that's what you think.'

Matteo left his chair to put both hands on the arms of hers, leaning over her, his eyes dark and passionate. 'You have no need to be afraid of me,' he told her huskily. '*Dio*, Grace, I realised there was always a chance it could happen again. I have had to come to terms with this possibility. But know this: it is not that I don't want another baby; it is only that I cannot bear the thought of losing you.'

'I know. And you won't.' Grace reached up to stroke his face with gentle fingers. 'Oh, Matteo, I want this baby— our baby—so much.'

'Do you think I don't?' Matteo breathed a little unevenly at the thought. 'But afterwards we will have some time alone together. I love my children, but I love my wife so very much...'

He kissed her then, supporting himself with his hands until Grace arched up to him, then he collapsed beside her on the lounger with a helpless groan. 'Have a care, *cara*,' he said. 'Our guests will be arriving for the party very shortly. Not least, your mother and your sisters. You would not wish for them to find us making love right here.'

Grace chuckled. 'I will if you will,' she said mischievously, and Matteo buried his face against her throat.

'Perhaps tonight I will not entertain your brothers-in-law,' he told her in a strangled voice. 'Tonight there will be no "headaches", eh, *cara*?'

Their daughter, Anna Maria, was born a little under eight months later, and once again Grace had had a fairly easy

confinement. So much so that when Matteo brought the
baby to her she was already anticipating the trip he had
promised months before.

They went to the Caribbean for their second honeymoon
six months later, leaving the *marchesa* and Grace's mother
in charge in their absence. It had been Matteo's idea that
Mrs Horton should winter in Valle di Falco, and for the
last two years she had occupied her own suite on the south
side of the villa.

Perhaps not surprisingly, she and the *marchesa* had become good friends, and there was no doubt that the warmer
climate was a boon to Mrs Horton's arthritis. But she still
spent the summer in England, catching up with her other
daughters and their families, and checking on the house in
Islington Crescent where Giles and Pauline still lived.

The trip to the Caribbean was heavenly. As well as
Matteo's satisfaction at having his wife all to himself,
Grace appreciated having her husband's undivided attention. At home, there was always some problem to be dealt
with. In Barbados, there was just sun and sea and love.

'By the way, Mum told me she'd heard from Pauline
that Julia got married last week,' Grace murmured sleepily,
relaxing in the aftermath of an afternoon making love. 'It
was apparently announced in the paper. Some businessman
or other, I believe.'

'Who cares?' groaned Matteo, grasping her hand when
it would have roamed down over his stomach. 'I'm grateful
to her for bringing us together, but nothing else.'

'Isn't it enough?' whispered Grace, finding it in her heart
to be charitable. She hoped Julia was happy. But no one
could be happier than she was herself...

"This book is DYNAMITE!"
—**Kristine Rolofson**

"A riveting page turner..."
—**Joan Elliott Pickart**

"Enough twists and turns to keep everyone
guessing... What a ride!"
—**Jule McBride**

See what all your favorite authors
are talking about.

Coming October 1999 to a retail store near you.

 **HARLEQUIN®**
Makes any time special ™

WIN A DREAM

In celebration of Harlequin®'s golden anniversary

Enter to win a *dream!* You could win:

- A luxurious trip for two to *The Renaissance Cottonwoods Resort* in Scottsdale, Arizona, or
- A bouquet of flowers once a week for a year from **FTD**, or
- A $500 shopping spree, or
- A fabulous bath & body gift basket, including **K-tel's** *Candlelight and Romance* 5-CD set.

Look for **WIN A DREAM** flash on specially marked Harlequin® titles by Penny Jordan, Dallas Schulze, Anne Stuart and Kristine Rolofson in October 1999*.

FTD

**RENAISSANCE.
COTTONWOODS RESORT**
SCOTTSDALE, ARIZONA

K·TEL

*No purchase necessary—for contest details send a self-addressed envelope to Harlequin Makes Any Time Special Contest, P.O. Box 9069, Buffalo, NY, 14269-9069 (include contest name on self-addressed envelope). Contest ends December 31, 1999. Open to U.S. and Canadian residents who are 18 or over. Void where prohibited.

PHMATS-GR

HARLEQUIN PRESENTS®

Seduction
SWEET REVENGE

They wanted to get even.
Instead they got...married!

by bestselling author

Penny Jordan

Don't miss Penny Jordan's latest enthralling miniseries
about four special women. Kelly, Anna, Beth and Dee
share a bond of friendship and a burning desire to
avenge a wrong. But in their quest for revenge, they
each discover an even stronger emotion.
Love.

Look out for all four books in Harlequin Presents®:

November 1999
THE MISTRESS ASSIGNMENT

December 1999
LOVER BY DECEPTION

January 2000
A TREACHEROUS SEDUCTION

February 2000
THE MARRIAGE RESOLUTION

Available at your favorite retail outlet.

HARLEQUIN®
Makes any time special ™

Coming Next Month

HARLEQUIN PRESENTS®

THE BEST HAS JUST GOTTEN BETTER!

#2061 THE MISTRESS ASSIGNMENT Penny Jordan
(Sweet Revenge/Seduction)
Kelly has agreed to act the seductress in order to teach a
lesson to the man who betrayed her best friend. It's a scheme
fraught with danger—especially when gorgeous stranger
Brough Frobisher gets caught in the cross fire....

#2062 THE REVENGE AFFAIR Susan Napier
(Presents Passion)
Joshua Wade was convinced that Regan was plotting to disrupt
their wedding. Regan had to admit there was unfinished
business between them—a reckless one-night stand.... She had
good reason for getting close to Joshua, though, but she could
never reveal her secret plans....

#2063 SLADE BARON'S BRIDE Sandra Marton
(The Barons)
When Lara Stevens and Slade Baron were both facing an
overnight delay in an airport, Slade suggested they spend the
time together. Who would she hurt if Lara accepted his
invitation? He wanted her, and she wanted . . . his child!

#2064 THE BOSS'S BABY Miranda Lee
(Expecting!)
When Olivia's fiancé ditched her, her world had been blown
apart and with it, her natural caution. She'd gone to the office
party and seduced her handsome boss! But now Olivia has a
secret she dare not tell him!

#2065 THE SECRET DAUGHTER Catherine Spencer
Soon after Joe Donnelly's sizzling night with Imogen Palmer,
she'd fled. Now ten years on, Joe was about to uncover an
astonishing story—one that would culminate in a heartrending
reunion with the daughter he never knew he had.

#2066 THE SOCIETY GROOM Mary Lyons
(Society Weddings)
When Olivia meets her former lover, rich socialite Dominic
FitzCharles, at a society wedding, he has a surprise for her: he
announces their betrothal to the press, in front of London's
elite. Just how is Olivia supposed to say no?